A Note to Readers

While the Allerton and Lankford families are fictional, the troubles faced by people living in Cincinnati during 1819 are all too true. For most of that year, the Ohio River was so low that boats couldn't travel on it. Many people lost their jobs, and families went hungry.

At that time, states printed their own money. The value of the money varied from day to day, and when there were financial problems, the money often became worthless. This confusing situation caused many problems that took more than a hundred years to straighten out.

Because there weren't radios or televisions, musical instruments were very important forms of entertainment for families in the 1800s. Having a piano or parlor organ in the home became common, and by the end of the century, most girls were expected to know how to play the piano at least a little.

TROUBLE
on the
OHIO RIVER

Norma Jean Lutz

BARBOUR
PUBLISHING, INC.
Uhrichsville, Ohio

To Gene and Barbara Yeager.
The two of you are the epitome of the fruit of the
Spirit gentleness. I cherish your friendship.

Published by Barbour Publishing, Inc.
P.O. Box 719
Uhrichsville, Ohio 44683
www.barbourbooks.com

Member of the
Evangelical Christian
Publishers Association

Printed in the United States of America.

Cover illustration by Matthew Archambault.
Inside illustrations by Adam Wallenta.

CHAPTER 1

Trouble at School

Excitement tumbled and bubbled deep inside ten-year-old Lucy Lankford's stomach, making it difficult for her to pay attention. Her chin rested on her hand as she stared out the schoolhouse window.

The crowded classroom on the first floor of the brick building was not only noisy, but stuffy. The classroom upstairs, where the older students attended, was just as crowded. Thankfully Lucy's seat was by an open window where she could feel the soft spring breeze blowing in. She didn't mind that she had to share a seat with Charlotte Hendricks. Charlotte had been her friend for almost two years.

April meant the school term was nearly over. That in itself was enough to make Lucy want to turn handsprings.

But today was much more exciting than the close of school. Tonight she and Mama would pen the order for her brand new piano.

She'd dreamed of having a piano for months. Finally Papa said, with the contracts for two new steamboats, there would be enough money for a piano. Lucy sighed as she thought of the pictures in the catalog she and Mama pored over night after night. But now the decision was made. Papa said the steamboat *Velocipede* would be leaving in the morning and the order would go onboard with the outgoing mail.

Shifting in the small hard seat, Lucy moved her attention to the front of the room, where Mr. Flinn tried his utmost to work on recitation with a group of the first- and second-grade students. Mr. Flinn's stand-up white collar, which that morning had looked starched and spiffy, now looked rather wilted. His black bow tie drooped as well.

Lucy had decided months ago that Oberlin Flinn was too kind and gentle to be a teacher, especially in this crowded room. The older boys talked out of turn and kept a ruckus rumbling most of the time. Last year's teacher, grouchy old Mr. Monfort, seemed harsh and mean, but at least the boys had behaved.

Out of the corner of her eye, Lucy saw Raggy Wallace shoot a spitwad right at the back of her cousin Ben's head. Ben Allerton sat two rows over with the sixth graders. Lucy watched as he reached up to remove the wet mass from his hair and turned around to scowl at Raggy. Even from two rows over, she could sense Ben's disgust. Ben had told her there were never boys like Raggy in his school in Boston.

Poor Ben. Ever since he'd arrived from Boston two months ago, several of the boys had made fun of his dapper clothes and Boston accent, but Raggy was the worst. As Mr.

Flinn turned his back, Lucy stuck her tongue out at Raggy, making Charlotte giggle. Raggy shook his fist at her and mouthed the threat "I'll get you."

Lucy just turned up her nose and ignored him. Charlotte nudged Lucy, then pinched her own nose, indicating that Raggy Wallace smelled bad. Lucy nodded in agreement. Raggy's dark hair was matted, his clothes worn and frayed, and his neck was the color of dirty dishwater. His nose seemed too long for his angular face. The boy was continually scratching, so Lucy was certain he must have lice.

On their shared slate, Charlotte and Lucy were supposed to be working their multiplication tables, but instead, Lucy had drawn a stick figure girl sitting at a piano. Charlotte knew all about the new piano that would soon be coming to the Lankford household and was happy for Lucy.

"I wouldn't even want a piano," Charlotte had said that day at recess time. "Then Mama would make me practice every day. I'd hate that." She screwed up her pretty face at the very thought.

But Lucy didn't see it that way. It was as though her fingers hungered to move over the smooth ivory keys and coax out melodies to accompany her singing.

Last year the church her family attended had purchased a piano. But only Widow Tuthill was allowed to go near the fine instrument. No one was supposed to touch the dark mahogany lid to take a peek at the even row of black and white keys. Lucy told Mama that was unfair. Mama just said, "Rules are rules, Little Lucy. You know that."

Now that Lucy had celebrated her tenth birthday, she hated being called "Little Lucy," but still Mama, Papa, and even her older brother, George, insisted on calling her that.

Just then, Mr. Flinn finished with the younger children

and called the class to order. His efforts were rewarded only slightly as the older boys continued to whisper and laugh. Raggy had a handful of followers who mimicked his every action, especially Willie Ashe and Gus Grosbeck.

"As we approach the closing of the school term," Mr. Flinn began, but he was interrupted with cheers from Raggy and those around him.

"Yea, hooray!" they cried in chorus. "No more school!"

Mr. Flinn's soft brown eyes were troubled as he surveyed the culprits. Tugging at his dark chin whiskers, he began again. "The superintendent of schools has asked that all classrooms have a presentation prepared for the closing day ceremony. Be thinking of how our classroom can contribute to the program, either individually or as a group."

Charlotte's hand shot up. When the teacher called on her, she said, "Lucy Lankford can sing, Mr. Flinn. She has the most beautiful voice in the world. Nicer than a nightingale."

Lucy felt herself blushing. She had no idea Charlotte was going to blurt out such a thing. Often she sang for family gatherings. A few times she'd even sung at church. Singing in front of the entire community would be quite different.

"Thank you, Charlotte." To Lucy, he said, "Would you please have a song prepared for the program, Lucy?"

"Yes, sir," she answered, feeling the giddiness building inside her. Now she had one more exciting thing to look forward to.

From the back of the room, Raggy said in a loud whisper, "Dapper-Dandy-Boston-Ben could show us how to talk Yankee talk."

Ben's cornsilk-colored hair didn't quite cover his ears, and Lucy saw them turn red right up to the tips. How she wished she could do something to cheer Ben. She tried to imagine what it would be like if she were to lose both her parents to such a wretched disease as yellow fever. That's what had happened to Ben just last winter.

Lucy turned to give Raggy her worst scowl. He was such a beast.

Mr. Flinn gave Raggy, whose name in class was Russell, a warning to keep silent, but the warnings carried little weight. Raggy did pretty much as he wanted. And that seldom meant schoolwork.

In the past, Raggy showed up for school only about half the time, but recently his attendance had become almost perfect. Lucy believed that Raggy came to school only to take part in tormenting poor, defenseless Ben.

At last, Mr. Flinn completed all the instructions regarding the school closing ceremonies, which, he said, would include a parade down Main Street. Charlotte and Lucy nudged one another at the prospect of a parade. What fun that would be!

Class was then dismissed, and Lucy went to the cloakroom to fetch her tin pail from the shelf. Ben was right there beside her. Out in the schoolyard, Charlotte called out goodbye as she and her older brother, John, headed west down Fourth Street toward their home. Lucy often wished Charlotte lived nearer Deer Creek so they could walk home together.

Before going out of the fenced schoolyard, Lucy said to Ben, "Wait a minute." Sitting down in the dirt, she proceeded to unbutton her hightop shoes and pull off her long, itchy woolen stockings. The shoes, which had been purchased at the shoemaker's last autumn, were now much too tight.

"Lucy, what are you doing?" Ben protested. "You can't walk barefoot in these filthy streets."

"Of course I can. Just watch me." She bounded to her

feet and wiggled her toes in the dirt, making little dust puffs. "Ah, now my feet are finally free."

Ben shook his head in disbelief. "No girl in Boston would walk home from school barefooted in the dirt." He paused a moment as he studied Fourth Street. It was nearly three inches deep in dirt. "But then, in Boston there're no dirt streets."

"Oh come on, Ben," she said hurrying on ahead of him and turning off Fourth Street to Walnut. "Forget about Boston for a while. Let's go down near the landing and look at the *Velocipede* before going home." Lucy wanted so much to help Ben forget about past things and for him to be as happy about Cincinnati as she was.

"I thought you weren't supposed to go near the landing by yourself," Ben countered, hurrying to catch up with her.

Lucy gave a little giggle. "I'm not by myself, silly. You're with me. And besides, we won't go all the way to the landing. We'll just look down from Second Street."

She knew Ben wanted to hurry home. Among other things, Ben was frightened of the many pigs that ran wild in the streets. The helpful pigs ate the garbage that was thrown into the streets every day by the town's residents.

"I know you're wary of the pigs, Ben," she told him as patiently as she could. "But we'll find two big old sticks, and if any pigs come along, we'll just whack them on the snout."

Lucy had never had a pesky pig attack her, but she knew other children had been attacked and seriously hurt. The gruesome stories had affected Ben.

She pointed to a yard where several large shade trees grew. "There should be a couple sticks under those trees." But before they could head that direction, out from between two buildings came Raggy along with Willie and Gus. They whooped and hollered.

"Henny, Penny, Benny! Dresses up in pretty clothes. Looks like a dandy!" Raggy called out in a singsong voice. Quickly the other two took up the chant.

"Henny, Penny, Benny! Looks like a dandy!"

Lucy caught the look of fear in Ben's eyes. These boys were more frightening to him than a whole herd of pigs.

Chapter 2
The Fight

Lucy stopped stock-still and turned about to glare at the trio. "You boys hush your mouths," she demanded. "Leave us alone."

Ben seemed confused. Lucy knew if he shot off running, they'd be after him for sure. "Pay 'em no mind at all, Benjamin Allerton," she said in a loud voice. "At least your name is better than 'Raggy.' " She spit out the word with all the disdain she could muster.

But Raggy's attention was not on Lucy. Coming closer, the tall boy reached down to grab a handful of the dirt from Walnut Street and flung it at Ben. "Now the dandy's a dirty, little dandy," he said, roaring with laughter.

"Stop that!" Ben protested. In vain he tried to brush off his nice navy coat and matching trousers. As Ben looked down at the mess, Raggy gave him a sudden shove, dumping him into the dirt.

Lucy could stand it no more. She began twirling around, swinging her tin pail as she went. Coming up right behind Raggy, she whammed him in the back of the legs with the pail. Raggy yowled with pain. The blow knocked him off balance, causing him to stumble. As he did, he grabbed one of Lucy's shoes that she'd dropped.

"Got your shoe," he hollered as he ran off, but Lucy was in hot pursuit.

"Stop that thief! He's a thief! Stop him."

Not looking where he was going, Raggy ran smack into a well-dressed gentleman with a top hat and pearl-handled cane. "Here, here, you ragamuffin," protested the man. "Watch where you're going."

"Stop him!" Lucy kept yelling. But Raggy threw the shoe as hard as he could and raced on down the street. His friends had long since disappeared.

With the help of the kind stranger, Lucy retrieved her shoe from within the high wrought iron fence of a fine home, then she retraced her steps back to where Ben stood waiting.

"You know, Ben," she said as she tried to catch her breath, "if we stick together, we can whip that terrible Raggy Wallace."

But even as she said it, she could tell Ben had no desire to whip anyone—even someone who'd pushed him into the dirt. It was as though there were no life in her cousin at all.

"Why do they allow ruffians like him to attend our school?" Ben wanted to know. "He should stay in Sausage Row where he belongs."

Ben was referring to the rundown district, near the landing, where the poorer people of the city lived.

"Papa says the city voted to pay the way for a few indigent children to attend as well as those of us who can pay the subscription." Lucy felt proud to know these facts, but it was only because she sometimes sat on the stair landing and listened to the grown-ups talk. She was always sent to bed before serious talk began.

"But why someone like Raggy?" Ben asked. "He doesn't even want to learn."

"It's because of the washerwoman he lives with. Mabel Peattie is her name. She took Raggy in when she found him roaming around Sausage Row all alone. I hear tell she's plumb set on him getting educated." Lucy chuckled. "They say she barged right into a meeting of the Board of Trustees to have her say."

Ben shook his head. "Doesn't she realize the boy's not worth it?"

"I guess not. You know, Ben, Reverend Corwin says we're supposed to love everybody, but I don't see how anyone could love that dirty, mean-mouthed Raggy."

As they talked, they approached the brink of the hill. Walnut Street, like most of the north-south streets in town, led down toward the public landing at the bank of the grand Ohio River.

Lucy loved the sight of the landing as it spread out before them. The wide cobblestone landing was flanked on the north by a row of stately buildings housing factories, mills, and warehouses that thrived on the river business. At one end of the landing was the brick factory, at the other end was the glassworks.

Situated on the far side of the glassworks was the Lankford

boatbuilding business in which Papa and George were involved. Papa had told her many times: "Lucy, someday you'll see dozens, and perhaps even scores, of steamboats plying these waters. And mark my word, the queen city of Cincinnati will be smack dab in the middle of it all!"

The awe and thrill in Papa's voice never failed to stir something inside of Lucy. How she wished Ben could be as impressed by this growing frontier city as she was.

"There it is," she cried out as they approached Front Street. "There's the *Velocipede*!" The queenly steamboat sat high and proud, docked in amongst the lesser keelboats, barges, and a few meager flatboats, which carried individual families and all their earthly belongings.

"You see steamboats most every day," Ben commented dryly. "Nothing to get worked up about."

"But this steamboat will carry the order for my new piano," she said, bouncing up and down on her bare toes.

Ben stopped beside her to study the river. "Why's the stern-wheeler out so far?" he asked.

Now Lucy stopped to look as well. "The water's low. Papa says it's because there was so little snow last winter, and so little rain this spring."

"What happens if the water goes lower?"

Papa and George had told Lucy about a summer many years ago when the river was dry for a number of months. But that was before they depended on steamboats to bring so many supplies from New York to the east and from New Orleans to the south.

"It won't go any lower," she assured him—and assured herself as well. "The spring rains will come soon. Just wait and see. Then, instead of complaining about the dust in the streets, you'll complain about all the mud." Lucy didn't even want to think about the prospect of a business slowdown on Cincinnati's public landing, especially if it meant a slowdown in the arrival of her piano.

The walk to Front Street had taken them a few blocks out of the way in their journey home. Before turning to walk back up the hill to Third, Lucy sat down to put on her shoes and stockings so Mama would never know.

Looking up at Ben, she asked, "Are you going to do something special for the school program, Ben?" She hopped up and they resumed their walk toward home.

Ben gave a shrug.

"You told me you learned Greek and Latin in Boston. Why don't you recite a piece in Greek?" She laughed as she thought of it. "That'd show that old Raggy a thing or two." But she could see her great idea sparked little response in Ben. If she could speak another language, she'd teach it to Charlotte. Then they could talk about Raggy and he'd never know what they were saying.

They were almost to the two-story brick home where Lucy lived on Symmes Street. She stopped a moment at their front gate, where her Mama had planted masses of rambling roses and honeysuckle bushes.

"In the morning Papa and I will take the order for my piano down to the steamboat," Lucy said. "If you want to go with us, come by earlier than usual."

Ben nodded in agreement. "Bye," he said, giving her a listless wave.

Lucy watched as he walked slowly toward the plank-covered log cabin situated in a clearing near Deer Creek. There Ben lived with his older brother, Richard; Richard's wife, Susannah; and the two little ones, Timothy and Pamela. Even though Richard had built on a loft for Benjamin, Lucy knew that, with two toddlers underfoot, it was a crowded place.

Opening the gate, she gave a sigh. It just didn't seem right that she should be so happy and Ben be so sad. Although Ben's bedroom in the loft was nice, no doubt it was still shabby in comparison to the fine room and fancy furnishings he'd enjoyed in Boston.

As she approached the front door, she could smell the wonderful aroma of her mama's beef stew. She burst into the big roomy kitchen, where Mama was bent over the butcher-block table stirring batter in a crockery bowl.

"Mama," she called out. "I'm home."

Mama looked up and brushed a strand of chestnut-colored hair from her forehead with the back of her hand. "Little Lucy, what happened to you? Your bonnet's down and your hair's a fright."

From the pantry, Lucy heard the snickers from Elora, their hired girl. Lucy ignored the snickers since it seemed Elora was always laughing at her. Quite honestly, Lucy had forgotten her bonnet had fallen back during her wild encounter with Raggy.

"Too much running at recess, I guess," she said quickly. She decided not to tell Mama about the chase, especially not while Elora was listening.

Just then, Elora emerged from the pantry carrying two pies. She was a thin girl with stringy hair and a mousey face. "Little Lucy is forever running," she said. "A few chores would settle her down, I'd say."

Elora accused Lucy of being petted because she was the youngest. If Lucy weren't so polite, she'd tell Elora that George called her an "addlepated girl with half the sense God gave a goose." Instead, she simply ignored Elora. Hugging her mother, she breathed deeply of the aromas of yeasty dumpling batter.

"Go wash your hands and brush your hair, then come and tell me about your day," said Mama.

Lucy pinched off a tiny bit of dough and popped it into her mouth. Her news couldn't wait until after a washing. "Mama," she said, "you'll never guess what. I'm going to sing at the school commencement exercises."

Mama stopped stirring batter now and raised her eyebrows. "Why, fancy that, our Little Lucy singing in front of all those people."

Elora came to take the bowl from Mama's hands and began dropping spoonfuls of the batter into the boiling stew.

"Mama, please," Lucy protested. "I'm not Little Lucy anymore. I'm ten years old." She leaned against the heavy butcher-block table and went back to her story. "It was because of Charlotte that I was asked. She told Mr. Flinn that I have a beautiful voice."

"And you certainly do." Mama waved her flour-covered hand. "Now go do as I said."

Backing away toward the kitchen door, Lucy added, "Will you and Papa help me chose the perfect song to sing?"

Mama nodded as she turned to dip her floured hands in a basin of water and wipe them on a linen towel. "We'll talk at supper," she said. "Go on now."

"And after supper we'll write out the piano order?"

Mama looked up and smiled her warm, kind smile. "That's exactly what we're going to do."

Lucy almost slipped and said she'd looked at the *Velocipede*, but she caught herself in the nick of time. She wasn't supposed to come home by way of Front Street.

Strolling out of the kitchen, Lucy gazed down the hallway

into the brand new parlor that Papa had built just last year. When it was finished, Mama had purchased flowered wallpaper at the mercantile store and had it hung, along with the heavy rust-colored drapes. Between the whatnot shelves and the fireplace by the tall windows was the very spot where Lucy's piano would sit. By using her imagination just a bit, she could actually see it sitting there and see herself running her fingers over the keys. She could even see pages and pages of music on the stand.

Halfway up the stairs, she hung out over the balustrade to again gaze at the empty space on the carpet where the piano would be placed. In just a few months it would be there. She could hardly wait!

CHAPTER 3
The Piano Order

The oil lamp made a warm golden glow in the center of the dining table as Mama laid out the quill, ink, sand, and paper. There, too, was the flickering candle to use as sealing wax.

"We'll work at the table," Mama said, "so we can sit together. There's room for only one person at the secretary."

All the fixings from dinner had been cleared away. Elora had gone home, taking a few of the leftovers with her in her wicker basket. Lucy was quite thankful that Elora did not live with them.

Mama spread out the catalog to the page they'd marked. "Now, you're sure this is the one?" she asked.

Lucy nodded, so excited she could barely speak. "I'm sure."

The handsome-looking piano was of mahogany and looked

every bit as nice as the one at church. Just let cranky Widow Tuthill have her old piano, Lucy thought. But she would never say such a thing out loud.

Mama picked up the quill to dip in the ink.

"May I, Mama? May I write the order?"

Mama looked surprised. "Why I suppose you can." She handed the quill to Lucy. "I'll read out the words and numbers."

Writing the order made Lucy feel just like a grown woman. Why couldn't Mama and Papa remember how grown up she was becoming?

When they were finished, Mama said, "Paul, would you come here a minute? We're all ready for the banknote."

Lucy's broad-shouldered Papa seemed to fill the room when he entered. He pulled out the other cane-bottomed chair and sat down.

"Let's see here now," he said, picking up the order. "My, my. Would you look at Little Lucy's graceful penmanship."

Lucy wanted to protest again about being called "little," but it seemed easier to say so to Mama than Papa. Papa always looked at her with a merry twinkle in his eye. "Thank you, Papa," she said instead.

"By the time the leaves turn and the pawpaws are ripe, we'll have a house filled with music."

"We already have a house filled with music, Papa," Lucy countered. "Your fiddle does that."

Papa reached out to gently pat her arm. "Now I'm trusting that you'll be making music much more grand than my screechy old fiddle."

Lucy laughed at his joke, but she thought his fiddle music was wonderful.

She watched as Papa's strong hand took the quill to write out the banknote for a partial payment. Because of Papa's successful boatbuilding business, he had a great deal of money now in the Branch Bank at Fourth and Vine.

"Ellie," she'd heard him say to Mama just last week, "when the two steamboats that George and I are building now are finished, we'll be just about as wealthy as Martin Baum."

The very thought made Lucy gasp. Mrs. Martin Baum had come to Mama's sewing circle one time. Lucy had never seen such an elegant and stylish dress as this lady of wealth had worn. Mr. Baum's landholdings in the city of Cincinnati were extensive. Charlotte's father also owned several prime lots along Fourth Street. Perhaps one day she and Papa and Mama would live in a fine house farther up on the hill.

"Here you go, Little Lucy," Papa said, handing her the note. Carefully she folded it inside the order and Mama helped her secure it with sealing wax. On the outside of the paper, she penned the address of the piano factory in Yonkers, New York, carefully wiping the quill when she was finished.

"This occasion calls for a celebration," Papa said. "What say we have a song before going to bed?"

Moving to the parlor, Papa took his fiddle down from the special shelf he'd made. After tuning the strings, he struck up a merry tune that he'd learned from a keelboatman. Lucy sang all the verses, with Mama and Papa joining in harmony on the chorus:

The boatman is a lucky man,
    No one can do as the boatman can,
The boatmen dance and the boatmen sing,
    The boatman is up to everything.
Hi-O, away we go,
Floating down the river on the O-hi-o.

Lucy rolled up the carpet and danced a jig as she'd seen the swarthy boatmen do. From her favorite spot on the bluff high above where Deer Creek emptied into the Ohio, she often watched the keelboats and the larger heavy barges moving up and down the river. Traveling upstream meant teams of muscular rowers must work the long oars. On top of the low boxy cabin sat the fiddler, sometimes wearing a slouch hat and a bright bandanna at his neck. The boatmen rowed to the rhythm of his music. But when the way was easy traveling downstream, the boatmen passed the time dancing jigs. The happy tunes and fancy steps stayed inside Lucy's head.

Mama laughed when they finished the last verse and the final rousing chorus. "When your piano is here, Lucy, perhaps our music will consist of something other than boatmen ditties."

Lucy nodded. "I'll learn church hymns, Mama," she agreed. "But I'll always love the happy boatmen songs."

Later as Papa opened the big family Bible and read the Scriptures, Lucy's thoughts turned to Ben's problem that day with Raggy Wallace. When they prayed, she asked Papa to say a special prayer for Ben to be happy.

Ben sat at the small table in the center of the cabin. Bent over his Latin textbook, he read the words by the flicker of the lamp. Timothy and Pamela were at last quietly sleeping in the trundle bed. When the little ones were awake, Ben found concentration impossible.

He tried to read several pages of Latin every evening. Sometimes if he had the time and the extra paper, he meticulously worked on translations. One time Susannah asked him why he worked so hard on his Latin studies, but Ben found he just couldn't explain it. "I like Latin" was all he said.

It was as though he owed it to his father, Benjamin, for whom he'd been named. His parents had made sure he had the finest education that Boston could offer; now it was up to him to maintain what he'd received. And it certainly wasn't going to happen at the crowded school he now attended.

Once he'd called it a charity school in front of Lucy, and she'd become upset. "It's not a charity school," she protested. "It's a public school. Papa pays subscription just like everyone else."

Ben hadn't meant to hurt his cousin's feelings, because he liked Lucy. But he knew the amount of subscription was a paltry sum. After all, the concept of the school was to cater to all—even creatures such as Raggy Wallace.

Ben's older brother, Richard, sat across from him, polishing and cleaning his musket and filling the room with the aroma of flaxseed oil. The small cabin seemed to shrink when Richard was there. His very presence loomed over Ben like a shadow. Because Richard had been impressed by the British and been away from home for so many years, Ben barely knew him. They were worlds apart. It was strange, but Ben felt more lonely when his brother was home than he did when he was away.

"Ben?" Susannah said softly. "It's time you were in bed."

"Yes, ma'am," Ben answered politely. Closing his book, he went to the basin near the cabin door, poured a little water from the pitcher, and washed his face and hands. There was lye soap nearby, but he hesitated to use it unless he was really dirty. He felt guilty using the family's supplies. His older brother had come to Cincinnati with nothing and had worked hard to eke out a living, and even now they had little to spare. Benjamin was just another mouth to feed.

As Ben moved to the ladder that led to his loft, Susannah came to put her arm about his shoulder. "Sleep well, Benjamin."

"Thank you."

Her touch, which felt so like his mother's, made hot tears burn in his eyes. He turned away and blinked them back.

Richard said, "Good night, Ben." But he never looked up from his prized gun.

Back home in Boston, when his parents were still alive, they closed each evening with Scripture reading and prayers. But Richard seemed to have forgotten all about God. Pulling off his waist shirt and breeches and pulling on his nightshirt, Ben wondered himself if God were still around.

Lying on his small cot, he stared through the semidarkness at the slanted roof just a few feet above his head.

Richard had many exciting stories to tell about his adventures with the British. When he'd escaped to Boston before leaving to come out West, Richard had said God had delivered him from his captors. If that were so, Ben wondered, why didn't Richard lead his family in prayers now?

From beneath his pillow Ben drew out the smooth piece of wood that he was carving with his sharp penknife. Father had told Ben many times that he had just the right touch to make a piece of wood come alive.

Now that the days were longer and light came in the small window, he carved and whittled after going to bed. But tonight he was too tired. Holding up the wood in the shadows of the loft, he smiled. The shape was that of a sleek codfishing schooner such as those docked in Boston Harbor. Carving the ship helped him to remember Boston.

Just then, he remembered he was to leave for school earlier the next morning. Climbing out of bed and moving to the ladder, he called down softly, "Susannah?"

"Yes, Ben?"

"Will you wake me earlier in the morning? I'm to go to the landing with Lucy and her father before school."

"I'll rouse you," Richard answered, "when I go out to cut the wood."

"Thank you," Ben said and returned to bed. Richard's words were like a slap. When Ben first arrived in Cincinnati, Richard had asked him to split kindling, but Ben had never swung an axe in his life. Although Ben was more than willing to learn, Richard had no patience to teach him.

"You might get those pretty clothes dirty," Richard had said.

The comment cut deeply. Ben had no other clothes to wear. While he'd seen many well-dressed men, especially around the business district of Fourth Street, he was dressed differently than most of the other boys.

In the low bureau at the foot of his cot were the portraits of Mother and Father. Father had commissioned them to be painted only a few months before they died. Sometimes Ben allowed himself to take them out and look. But very rarely. And only when he was alone. He never wanted his brave older brother to see him cry.

He had very nearly cried that afternoon when Raggy attacked him. In the darkness, he smiled as he remembered the sight of Lucy swinging her tin pail with all her might.

While Ben hated having a girl stand up for him, still and all, he appreciated Lucy's friendship. He knew she was on his side. She didn't have to invite him to come to the steamboat with her in the morning. He would have to remember to thank her for her kindness.

Being near a steamboat might remind him of the sad journey down the Ohio a few months ago. He'd have to be careful and not cry. Again.

CHAPTER 4

News from the Landing

A light patter of rain was falling when Lucy heard Ben's knock at the kitchen door the next morning. He was early. She and Mama and Papa hadn't yet finished breakfast.

Lucy left her place at the table to answer his knock. "Come in," she said. Ben's solemn face lit up as he smelled the aroma of Mama's flapjacks.

"Good morning, Ben," Mama called out. Without asking, Mama fetched another plate from the cupboard. "You might as well have a few flapjacks and a slice of ham while you wait."

Ben sat down at the table without being asked twice. By the time Lucy had gone upstairs to fetch her cloak with the hood, Ben had polished off the plate of food. Lucy wondered if he'd had much breakfast at Richard's house.

She'd heard George and Papa talking about Richard. When Richard had first arrived in Cincinnati, he'd worked at the boatworks for a short time but then decided to go out on his own as a tanner. What he didn't take into account was that there were already more than a dozen tanyards and no need for a new one. He hadn't done as well as he'd hoped, so Papa had offered to let him come back to the boatworks. Richard turned down the offer. Papa told George, "Richard is too proud."

Maybe Richard didn't have enough money to feed Ben properly. That thought worried Lucy. Richard worked some days at the tanyard. Other days he chopped wood and went hunting in the nearby forests.

She learned these things while sitting on the stair landing to listen to the grown-ups talk. She wondered when Mama and Papa would ever realize that she was old enough to be included in the grown-ups' talk.

"Thank you, Mrs. Lankford," Ben told Mama, as he followed Papa and Lucy out the door.

"Please, Ben," Mama called after him. "You may call me Aunt Ellie."

"Yes, ma'am," Ben called back. "Yes, ma'am, Aunt Ellie."

Lucy figured there wasn't a more polite boy than Ben in all the state of Ohio.

The landing was a busy place. Horses whinnied as they pulled wagons full of boxes, bags, and barrels close to the boat for unloading. Black stevedores shouted to one another and tossed about heavy bags of flour as though they were feather pillows. Several fine carriages, harnessed with smart-stepping horses, were hitched nearby as passengers said good-bye to friends and family in preparation to embark.

Papa was a friend of the captain of the *Velocipede*, so he strode up the broad gangplank as though he had a ticket to ride all the way to Pittsburgh. Captain Sorley Saffins was down on deck, greeting passengers and overseeing the loading so all was done in an orderly manner.

"Top o' the morning to you, Paul Lankford," Captain Saffins called out when he saw Papa. Lucy liked the captain's cheery voice, his ruddy red cheeks, and his broad thick mustache. "And here's Little Lucy, too. To what do I owe this special visit?"

After introducing Ben to the tall captain, Papa explained, "Lucy has a letter to go in the mailbag, Captain Saffins."

The captain raised his bushy eyebrows. "Now it must be terribly important to be hand-delivered to the captain."

Lucy was bursting to tell. She held up the folded and sealed letter. "It's my order for a new piano. It's coming from a factory in New York."

"Is that a fact?" The captain reached out his large, big-boned hand. "I'll see to it that it's delivered safely." He slipped the order into the pocket of his greatcoat with its shiny brass buttons. Looking wistfully out at the river, he added, "If we don't get a little rain, we may not see you again until this time next year."

Hearing those frightful words, Lucy stopped still. But then came Papa's reassuring voice. "See those clouds?" Papa waved to indicate the overcast skies. "The Lord willing, the spring rains will come. And probably too much, as usual. That's the way it seems to happen around here."

Captain Saffins shook his head. "I want to think you're right, Mr. Lankford, but. . ." Just then, the captain's attention was diverted. "Hey there!" he yelled out to a carriage that had just pulled up and blocked the loading area. "Excuse me, folks. I must go see about this." And he was gone.

Lucy turned around to see Ben standing by the deck railing, running his fingers gently over the carved and polished wood. There was that sad look on his face again. Adjusting her tin pail on her arm beneath her long cloak, she went over to stand beside him.

"Do you like steamships?" she asked.

"I suppose so. That is, I like the way they're made. Especially the fancy woodwork."

Papa walked up behind them. "Time for you two to scoot off to school."

Lucy looked up at Papa. "But I wanted to say good morning to George since we're so close. May I please, Papa?"

Lucy's older brother, George, was one of her favorite persons in the whole world. When George took pretty Patricia for his bride, Lucy wept. She was jealous of Patricia for taking George away from her. But now the hurt was almost gone. Sometimes she was allowed to go to George and Patricia's new home and stay overnight. That was fun.

Papa was looking at her with a twinkle in his eye. "Only if you promise to stay just a moment, then run on to school. You don't want to be responsible for making Ben late."

Following Papa's long strides down the wide cobblestone landing, Lucy looked through the raindrops at the row of tall three- and four-story buildings that lined the landing. Each one was home to a thriving business. She wanted to comment on them to Ben, but she saw he wasn't noticing them at all. Ben was glancing wistfully back at the steamboat.

At the boatworks, the skeletal frames of the two new steamboats were taking shape. Nearby stood a large building where George oversaw the work on the steam engines.

George was standing outside, talking to the men who were working on the boat frames.

When Lucy called out to him, he turned. Running to lift her up and swing her around, he said, "Little Lucy! What are you doing at the landing? This is a school morning."

Once he'd set her down, Lucy explained about the order for her brand new piano.

"Ah, so you're finally getting your piano? Papa's little pet," he teased. "I suppose if you wanted the scepter from the king of Prussia, he'd get it for you."

"Oh, George, that's not true. When I learn to play, the piano will be for all the family. You can come and listen."

George screwed up his face and stuck his fingers in his ears. "And listen to you play sour notes? Not on your life."

She started to smack at him but couldn't get her arm out of her cloak before he jumped, laughing, out of her reach.

Papa had been talking to his workers, but now he turned to tell Lucy and Ben to get on their way. "You'll have to hurry now."

"Yes, Papa." Lucy turned to see Ben picking up scrap pieces of wood and slipping them into his pocket. Ben was handy with his penknife. She'd seen the whistles and tops he'd carved for Timothy and Pamela.

"Come on, Ben," she hollered to him. "I'll race you up the hill."

If Ben really tried, Lucy was sure he could easily win the race. But he gave the race only a half-hearted try. By the time they reached the schoolhouse, huffing and puffing, the gray clouds had broken apart and the warm sun was out.

Later that morning at recess, Lucy told Charlotte about the incident the day before with Raggy.

"How I wish you walked home the same direction as

31

John and I," Charlotte said. "With John around, Raggy would never bother you."

Lucy knew that was true. Even though Raggy Wallace was big for his age, Charlotte's older brother, John, was bigger. How nice it would be to have a guardian nearby like John Hendricks.

"Mama says," Charlotte confided, "that when Raggy was younger, he helped deliver wash for Mabel Peattie. Now all he does is run loose all over town and cause mischief."

Mabel was the washerwoman for Charlotte's family, so Charlotte would know. Lucy shook her head at the thought of dirty, lazy Raggy. "And helping Mabel with the deliveries is the least he could do for being allowed to live in the lean-to behind her shack."

Tiring of talking about Raggy Wallace, they turned their conversation to the school program and the pretty new dresses they would wear.

"If I was having to stand before the entire city to sing," Charlotte said, "I'd be petrified."

"I'm excited," Lucy said, "but I'm not afraid." It was difficult to explain just how much she loved singing in front of people.

Suddenly, loud shouts sounded from a far corner of the playground. Looking that direction, Lucy felt her heart sink. Raggy, Willie, and Gus had Ben cornered near the fence and were taunting him. Other boys stood around laughing. Lucy hated the onlookers for not helping Ben.

"Come on, Charlotte," she said. "Ben needs our help."

"You go," Charlotte said. "I have an idea."

Without a look back, Lucy ran quickly toward Ben, yelling at the boys to get away and leave him alone.

Raggy stopped and glared at her. "Fellows, this little

wildcat-gal's the one that smacked me on the legs."

"Yes, and I'd do it again quick as you can draw a breath, Raggy Wallace," Lucy told him.

With attention shifted away from him, Ben tried to make a break, but Gus and Willie blocked his escape. "Oh no you don't, dapper boy," Gus mocked.

Raggy gave a raspy laugh and spit a stream of 'baccy juice, as he called it. "Our fancy boy here needs a little gal to come rescue him. Tsk, tsk," he said through his teeth. "Ain't that a sight?"

Just as Lucy despaired that nothing but the recess bell could save Ben, a shout sounded behind her. "Get on out of here, you no good scalawags."

John Hendricks was striding forcefully toward Raggy, and following him was Charlotte, sporting a wide grin!

CHAPTER 5
Lidell's Mercantile

At the sight of the taller, stronger boy coming toward them, Willie and Gus fled. Raggy stood his ground for a moment, calling after his pals not to run, but it was no use. They were gone.

"Go on," John said to Raggy. "Slither out of here like your two snaky friends. And in the future, pick on someone your own size."

"Just you wait." Raggy shook his fist at Ben, whose face was white as a bedsheet. "I'll get you when you ain't got no little gal to hide behind." With that he ran off to another part of the schoolyard.

"Well, what're you looking at?" John said sternly to the other boys standing about. Suddenly the crowd melted away.

Once Ben could find his voice, he thanked John.

"Think nothing of it," John said smiling.

"I don't know why those boys dislike me so," Ben said, his voice still shaky. "I've done nothing to harm them."

John laughed. "That has nothing to do with it, my friend. Ruffians like that are always looking for fresh prey. You just happen to be it."

Ben shook his head as though he couldn't believe it.

"You're from Boston as I remember it." John had his arm about Ben's shoulder and was leading him to a shade tree where they sat down on the grass. "Surely you had Raggy's kind in Boston."

"Not where I lived," Ben said quietly.

"Well, let me tell you about boys like Raggy. All you have to do is stand your ground and they'll hightail it. Every time."

While Ben politely thanked John Hendricks for the advice, Lucy could see he wasn't truly convinced. It was just like when she told him that a smart smack on a pig's snout would send it running. He simply didn't believe her.

The clanging of the bell broke into the conversation, and soon they were standing in their straight lines, ready to march to their classrooms. Lucy gave Charlotte a wink and a grin as they saw Raggy trailing at the end of the line. With a friend like John Hendricks, Lucy reasoned, perhaps Ben would learn to laugh and have some fun.

Saturday was Lucy's favorite day of the week. No school meant she could go to the market with Mama. The busy marketplace was filled with wagonloads of meat and produce from the outlying farms. Lucy loved the sights and sounds and the hustle and bustle. Often she'd asked for permission to do the market shopping alone. "I can do it, Mama," she'd say. "I've watched you, and I know how to find the firmest heads of cabbage and the plumpest plucked hens."

But Mama always said no. "You're too little to shop alone. Some of the merchants in the market can't be trusted."

But this week, Lucy tried a new approach. She asked that Ben go along and that Mama allow the two of them to do the shopping. "Perhaps Ben can make purchases for Susannah." Once Lucy saw she had Mama's full attention, she added, "Susannah would surely welcome such help.

When at last Mama gave in and reluctantly gave permission, Lucy realized she'd not even asked Ben. When she did ask him, he seemed willing enough. At least Lucy was right about Susannah.

"What a relief it will be not to have to make my way through the crowds with two little ones in tow," she said.

So it was settled. Before dawn on Saturday morning, Ben was at the Lankford's back door with Susannah's list in his hand and a basket on his arm. Mama instructed Lucy several times about how to dicker for the best prices.

"When you've finished at the market," she added, "please stop at Lidell's Mercantile for a paper of pins and a yard of sprigged muslin."

To the store as well! Lucy could hardly believe her good fortune. This made her feel more grown up than ever.

The sky behind the hills to the west of the city showed barely a smudge of pink as Ben and Lucy walked toward the lower market. A broad roof covered most of the area between Main and Sycamore and was supported by triple rows of brick pillars. But the sides were all open.

Since Ben had never before seen an open-air market,

Lucy showed him around and introduced him to the merchants she knew. Many of the farmers drove their wagons through the dark of night to vie for prime positions at the market. Feeling quite important, Lucy taught Ben how to squeeze the cabbages to be sure they were not rotten in the center.

"Wait until summer when the grapes come in," she told him as she chose a fat hen hanging from the racks. Talking about the juicy grapes made her mouth water. "There will be great baskets full of them, and you eat until you cannot eat any more."

"I'm not sure Susannah's budget could purchase that many grapes," Ben commented.

Lucy wanted to say that Richard could earn fine wages at the boatworks, but she held her tongue. After all, Ben wasn't responsible for Richard's actions.

At Mr. Van Ruys's wagon, she found the firmest cabbages, and at Mr. Hempel's wagon, she purchased the eggs. In her basket was a linen towel in which she was to wrap the eggs. Just as they were walking back through the rows of jammed-in wagons, Lucy whispered, "Look there, Ben. It's Raggy Wallace."

Raggy was slinking about the edges of the market area. As they watched, he slipped up to the back end of a wagon, reached in to grab a large white turnip, and then fled.

Lucy gave a loud whoop and pushed through the crowd in that direction. "Stop that boy! He's a thief." But no one was quick enough, and Raggy was long gone.

Leaving the market, they walked up Main toward Fourth Street and Lidell's Mercantile. Muttering under his breath, Ben said, "It must be awful to have to steal for food."

Lucy looked over at Ben in surprise. He sounded almost

as though he felt sorry for Raggy. She knew she'd never steal, no matter how little she had. Wanting to change the subject, she said, "Mama gave me enough extra for each of us to have a stick of peppermint. You like peppermint, don't you?"

"Who wouldn't like peppermint?" he answered dully.

Lucy was convinced nothing could ever excite Ben.

The heavy door of the mercantile was propped open, but the fresh spring air couldn't soften the strong mixtures of aromas inside the store. Here one could find everything from axe heads and kegs of nails to buggy whips and bolts of cloth. The store was fairly bristling with business.

Once inside, Lucy was surprised to see John Hendricks with a broom in his hands sweeping the wooden floor. When he greeted them with a smile and a wave, Lucy noticed that Ben brightened some.

"Charlotte never told me you worked for the Lidells," Lucy said.

"I just started today." John waved his hand at all the merchandise and added, "Until I learn where everything is, I'm doing odd jobs. But soon I'll be a clerk." There was a note of pride in his voice. "Hey, Mr. Lidell," he called over to a scar-faced man behind the counter. "We have a couple of customers here."

"Hi Lucy, Ben," Charles Lidell greeted them cheerily. "What can I do for you today?" In spite of his terribly scarred face, Charles was a kind man and was a dear friend of Lucy's brother, George.

Lucy pulled out her list. "Mama needs a paper of pins and a yard of sprigged muslin."

"Pins and muslin, coming right up," he said. Pulling down the bolt of cloth and laying it on the counter, Charles asked, "How's George doing these days? I don't see him much anymore."

"He and Papa are working hard to finish the two steamboats as soon as possible. Mama says they barely take time to breathe."

Charles chuckled at her comment. Carefully he measured and cut the muslin, folding the piece and returning the bolt to the shelf. "Now just tell me what those big old boats are gonna float on?" he asked. "From the looks of things, the river'll be down to a trickle in a few more weeks."

Lucy didn't want to hear those words. True, there still hadn't been any hard spring rains, but they would come. She was sure of it. "Papa says the spring rains are just late," she told Charles.

"Late, huh? Well, I guess the snows were late, too. Don't forget, Little Lucy, there was very little snow all winter. Maybe the snows will come in June to raise the river level," he joked.

Lucy quickly changed the subject. "Ben and I would each like a peppermint stick as well, please."

"Two peppermint sticks." He added the items to the list, then took the wide-mouth jar from a shelf and brought it down to the counter where they could choose their own.

After Lucy paid Charles, Ben suggested they put the cloth and pins in his basket since it wasn't as full as hers.

"Good idea," Lucy agreed. "Now let's get on home and show Mama what a good job we've done."

As they went out the door, John called out, "Has Raggy Wallace bothered you anymore?"

Lucy answered by telling him they'd seen Raggy swiping vegetables at the market only a few moments earlier.

John nodded. "I'd suspect no less of the ruffian." Giving

the broom a couple more swipes, he added, "Remember now, Ben, what I told you about the likes of Raggy."

Ben nodded. "Yes, John. Thank you."

Lucy was anxious to get home to see the pleased look on Mama's face. Elora could not have done as well. Perhaps now Mama would no longer call her "Little Lucy."

As they walked down the hill, Lucy asked Ben what he thought of the market, but his comments were vague. Sometimes Lucy wished she could do things and go places with fun-loving Charlotte rather than glum Ben. Charlotte and she would have giggled and laughed throughout the entire morning.

Just as they were ready to turn the corner at Fourth and Main, she heard Ben give a groan. "Oh no," he said. "Not again."

Raggy Wallace was coming toward them with a menacing scowl on his face.

"I heard you calling me a thief at the market awhile ago," Raggy said.

"I called you a thief, because you are a thief," Lucy retorted.

"Don't make him any madder," Ben muttered, stopping in his tracks.

"So the Boston dandy goes to market with his little basket on his arm," Raggy taunted as he drew nearer. "Let's see what dapper-boy buys at the market." Bumping into Lucy, Raggy grabbed at Ben's basket, yanking out the piece of muslin.

Lucy nearly fell, but righted herself just in time. She could only hope no eggs were broken. Raggy whipped out the cloth and draped it over his dirty hair. In a singsong voice, he said, "Oh look, I'm dressed like the dandy from Boston."

"Give that back," Lucy demanded. "That's my mama's cloth. I'll call the watchman on you."

Raggy was dancing about, raising a cloud of dust beneath his feet and having a great time with his own jesting. "Now there's no big boy to save you," he taunted, waving the cloth in the air.

Lucy knew the watchman who held this area was a tall, friendly man named Mr. Pike. If only. . .

Suddenly, at the top of her voice, she began to scream as though she were dying. "Help, help, Mr. Pike! We're being robbed!"

"Hush that caterwauling," Raggy demanded.

But Lucy wouldn't stop. She screamed and hollered and yelled and stamped her feet. "Give me back that muslin," she yelled. "You terrible no-good thief." Curtains rustled at windows as people peered out. Mr. Pike came running up the hill toward them, with his large rattle-stick in his hand. As soon as Raggy spied him, he threw the sprigged muslin in the dirt and ran down a side street as fast as he could go.

"I'm sorry, Lucy," Ben said as he picked up the cloth and shook out the dust.

"What's going on here?" Mr. Pike demanded. He was panting heavily from his uphill sprint. "Oh it's you, Lucy Lankford. How are you, young lady?"

"Not very well, Mr. Pike. That mean, old boy tried to take our things we bought at the market."

"Come on," Ben said to Lucy. "There's nothing he can do now."

"Who?" Mr. Pike wanted to know. "What boy?"

"Raggy Wallace is his name," Lucy told him.

Mr. Pike nodded. "I know him. He's the boy who lives with Mrs. Peattie."

41

"That's the one," Lucy said. Ben was beginning to walk on down the hill. "Ben, wait for me," she called out.

"All the watchmen from here down to the public landing have chased that boy at one time or other," Mr. Pike told her. "But I'll keep my eye out."

"Well, he didn't really take anything, Mr. Pike. I mean," she tried to explain as she started walking after Ben, "he did take something, but he gave it back again."

Mr. Pike nodded. "I'll keep an eye out just the same."

"Thank you, Mr. Pike," Lucy called back as she chased to catch up with Ben. When she was beside him again, she asked, "Why'd you say you were sorry awhile ago? You didn't do anything."

"I know," Ben said, his eyes sad. "That's why I apologized. I didn't do anything."

CHAPTER 6

Last Day of School

Ben said good-bye to Lucy at the front gate and politely thanked her for inviting him to go along. "I really did enjoy the market," he told her, "and the peppermint stick."

"You're welcome, Ben. See you tomorrow at church."

He nodded and went on his way.

When Lucy presented to Mama the basket containing one cracked egg and a yard of dirty sprigged muslin, Elora said to Mama, "I knew you should never have let her go to the market alone. She's just too little."

Lucy glared at the hired girl. "I am not too little. There's a boy named Raggy Wallace who torments Ben terribly. He tried to take Ben's basket and he pushed me. We saw him stealing turnips in the market."

"The boy would never have bothered you if I'd been with you," Elora put in. "Or your mama."

Sometimes Lucy wished Elora didn't work for them. She could help Mama with some of the work, if only Mama would let her.

"How was it you were able to get the cloth back?" Mother asked in a kind voice. It was good to know she wasn't angry at Lucy.

"Mr. Pike, the watchman, heard me yelling and came running."

"Why didn't this bad boy named Raggy just run off with the cloth? Why did he throw it down?"

Mama's question surprised Lucy. She shook her head. "Because if he kept it, Mr. Pike would have run after him and he would have been a thief."

"But you say he stole turnips?" Mama took the items from the basket and began putting them away.

Lucy didn't understand what Mama was getting at, nor did she want to know. Raggy Wallace was a mean, horrible boy, and that's all there was to it. "He stole the cloth, then threw it in the dirt," she said, trying to make the story worse. "He pushed me so hard, that if I'd fallen, your cabbages and turnips would have been full of dirt and the eggs all broken."

"I believe at prayers tonight, we shall pray for Raggy Wallace," Mama said. "Now go to your room and freshen up. We'll have cabbage wedges with our salt pork for lunch."

Not only did Mama pray for Raggy that night, she also instructed Lucy to pray for him at church the next morning. Now that was going to take some doing!

On Sundays they walked to church with Richard and Susannah and little Timothy and Pamela. Lucy's bonnet was new. The ruffles and ribbons fascinated two-year-old Pamela.

"Pitty ribbon," she said, wanting to touch the bonnet. Lucy adored the cute little Pamela with her mop of copper-colored curls.

Timothy held tightly to Ben's hand, and Lucy noted how the little boy dogged the steps of his young uncle. Richard, as usual, had little to say. Lucy couldn't imagine being as quiet as Richard Allerton. What a chore that would be. Mama and Susannah, on the other hand, always chatted non-stop.

As they entered the sanctuary, Widow Tuthill was seated at the piano, playing a grand hymn. Before the piano had arrived, Lucy hated her family's second-row pew, but now she was thankful. Lucy watched every move Widow Tuthill made as her fingers scooted over the glossy keys, amazed at the combination of sounds that came out. Someday she would know how to create lovely music on her very own piano.

The Reverend Corwin's message lasted for several hours. Sometimes there would be a break, during which they sang hymns from the hymnbooks. If Lucy had her way, they'd sing for hours and take a break to listen to a short sermon!

Although Lucy listened only half-heartedly, at one point she heard the Reverend say that it was God's will that all should come to repentance. That God willed no one to perish or be lost. Could that include people like Raggy and the riffraff that lived by the landing in Sausage Row? Then the Reverend Corwin added, "By our love and our example, we draw others into the kingdom."

After church, Lucy thought about what those words meant. No matter how she twisted and turned it around in her head, she just couldn't see any way she could love Raggy Wallace or set an example for him. She wanted to bean him on the head and make him leave Ben alone forever.

The day of the school commencement exercises broke sunny and bright. Lucy wanted more than anything to enjoy every moment of the day, but the conversation she'd overheard the night before between Papa and George kept ringing in her ears. There still hadn't been a drop of rain, and the low river level meant no barges, no keelboats, and no steamboats. Lucy had never seen the beautiful Ohio River so low. That in itself was scary enough.

But sitting quietly on the stair landing, she'd heard Papa and George talking about yet another problem—the Cincinnati banks.

"They've extended too much credit," Papa said.

"But all banks out West have operated on credit," George protested. "There's no other way to make it go."

"Yes," Papa answered in a low voice, "but all cities aren't suffering from lack of river traffic. It would be a double blow for us if the banks fold."

For the first time ever, Lucy left off listening and crept back into bed. What did it mean to have the banks fold? Did that mean the banknote Papa wrote for the piano would not be any good?

She and Charlotte were standing in front of the schoolhouse. They were in their proper position, along with hundreds of other students, waiting for the parade to begin. All of Fourth Street was decked out in bunting and banners. Lucy reckoned most of the city had turned out for the occasion. It felt nice, and a little strange, to feel the warm sun on her head and face. But none of the girls wore their bonnets, and the boys had left their caps off. All the children were to be bareheaded, wear light-colored clothing, and wave streamers as they proceeded down the broad street, singing as they went.

With a pounding of the bass drum and clash of cymbals, the band struck up a lively tune and the parade was underway. Lucy marched and sang and waved her streamer with all the others. At the corner of Fourth and Broadway, she saw Papa and Mama standing at the curbing with George and Patricia. She smiled to them and waved her streamer with more enthusiasm. It was good to see Papa smiling. There'd been worry lines on his brow for many weeks.

The parade led to the town square, where the children were seated on the grass. On the bandstand stood Isaac Allan, superintendent of the city schools, who called the crowd to attention. Acting as master of ceremonies, Mr. Allan announced the special presentations from each classroom.

When it was Lucy's turn, she stood and walked proudly to the platform. The leader of the band put his pitch pipe to his lips to give her the correct key. Looking out over the thousands of faces, she searched for Mama and Papa. When at last she spied them standing beneath a sprawling oak tree, she sang to Papa the clear sweet melody of "A Mighty Fortress Is Our God." A hush fell over the crowd as the words of comfort touched fearful hearts. Coming to the second verse, she sang:

Did we in our own strength confide
    Our striving would be losing.
Were not the right man on our side,
    The Man of God's own choosing.
Dost ask who that may be?
    Christ Jesus, it is He
Lord Sabaoth His name

From age to age the same
And He must win the battle.

Even as she sang, Lucy wondered if Jesus would help them win their battle against the awful problems of a dry river and banking systems that were falling apart. Could she be as certain as the hymn stated?

After the presentations, speeches, and prayers were completed, there were games and picnics beneath the cool shade of the trees in the square. Mama had brought Lucy's school bonnet along, but no one else was wearing one, so she convinced Mama to let her run bareheaded throughout the afternoon.

She introduced Charlotte and John to her family. John politely invited Ben to join in the races and games with him and his friend. Lucy was surprised and pleased when Ben agreed.

Charlotte's little sister, Mercy, was a toddler near Pamela's age. Charlotte and Lucy had great fun walking around among the crowds with the toddlers in tow. Thankfully, Raggy had not appeared that day. Nor had she seen Willie or Gus.

As they sat in the grass near the bandstand, listening to the rousing band music, Lucy mentioned the boys' absence to Charlotte.

Pulling Mercy into her lap, Charlotte said, "But they're the indigent students, remember?"

"What do you mean?"

"Lucy, think about it. Can you imagine their dirty clothes in the parade along with all the pretty linen dresses and the other boys' white shirts and nice bow ties? Why they don't even have shoes."

Lucy felt silly that she'd not thought of that before. It

was true. When snow was on the ground, Raggy wore a pair of boots that looked as though they'd been cast off by someone much larger than he. As soon as the frost was off, he was barefoot again. What shoes would he have worn in the parade?

Suddenly, Lucy felt a little ache deep in the pit of her stomach. An ache she couldn't explain, and one that didn't want to go away.

CHAPTER 7

Ben's Challenge

Whippoorwills echoed their lonely calls in the trees above Ben's head. The dense grove of buckeye, sycamore, and honey locust trees blocked out the dimming June sky. Only through a few patches in the leafy boughs could he see the stars beginning to come out. Beside him Lucy sat quietly as she stared down the bluff at the wide muddy bog that was once a rushing river. The ferries that used to carry folks back and forth from the Kentucky side to the Ohio side were land-locked and useless.

It wasn't like Lucy to be still or even to sit still. Ben knew she was worried about her family. And he was worried as well. The saddest thing to Ben was that Lucy never mentioned her piano anymore. Had she lost hope?

If Ben hadn't liked Cincinnati when he first arrived, he liked it even less now. The entire city seemed to be falling apart. Land prices had caved in and factories were closing their doors. He understood some of what was happening, but most he did not.

"It's not just the lack of river traffic is it?" he said to Lucy, breaking the silence.

Lucy turned to him. Her bonnet hung down her back by its ribbons. "You mean why the businesses are failing? No, Ben, it's not just the river."

Ben brushed leaves off his homespun trousers. After school let out, Susannah had found some old clothes of Richard's and cut them down for Ben. The feel of linsey-woolsey took some getting used to, but at least he would no longer be called a dandy. "I've asked Richard about things, but he won't talk."

"Same with Papa," Lucy agreed. "He says I'm too young to understand. But I've heard plenty of talk between him and George and with Mama, too." She pulled at the tuft on a purple thistle weed. It broke apart in her hands. "I heard Papa call it a 'depression.' He says now that Americans are trading with the British rather than fighting with them, British products are cheaper than our products. That puts American factories out of business."

Ben thought about that for a minute. "But the banks. . ."

"I don't understand, either. All I know is that the banknotes that used to be worth something aren't worth anything now."

"Richard said he was glad he didn't have any money in a worthless old bank."

"This is one time your brother may be right."

Ben looked away for fear he might see Lucy cry. When

she spoke again, Lucy said, "Papa and George both trusted the bank, and now they have nothing. And the money they expected to receive from the sale of the boats won't be coming. The buyers can't come downriver to fetch them." Pulling her hankie from her apron pocket, Lucy blew her nose. "Papa doesn't even know if the owners still have the money to buy the boats."

After a moment, Ben tried to change the subject. "Richard wants me to go hunting with him."

Lucy brightened a bit, tucking her hankie back in her pocket. "That's good, Ben. At least you'll be helping. I wish I could do more to help."

"I'm sort of afraid of the musket."

Lucy nodded. "You can get over being afraid."

"Do you think so?" Ben sometimes envied Lucy's fearlessness.

"Richard may not talk much, but I imagine he'll be a good teacher."

Ben thought about that. "He's not very patient. I mean, he's not very patient with me. He's pretty patient with Timothy and Pamela."

"That's because they're his own. That's different. He probably expects more of you because you're older."

"When he's gone from the house, I've been practicing splitting kindling."

"Have you?" Lucy's look of surprise pleased Ben. "I'm proud of you. How're you doing?"

"Not too well, but I'm not giving up. Susannah's helping me keep the secret."

"I've been lending a hand around the house more, too, since Mama had to let Elora go." She gave a little laugh. "I used to wish Elora didn't work for us. Now I'm sorry I had those thoughts. Elora needed the work and Mama needed her help."

"You couldn't have known how things were going to change."

"I know, but I'm still going to be more careful about my thoughts." Methodically, she pulled the ribbons of her bonnet through her fingers. "I wish we could do more, Ben. I wish we could help somehow."

Ben knew what she meant. Now that circumstances in the city had seen a downturn, Ben felt even more guilty for eating at Richard's table. Many nights he ate only half of his portion and made sure Timothy and Pamela took the rest. Then he went to bed dreaming of the heavy-laden table at his old home back in Boston. There were delicacies there, such as his mother's rhubarb pies, which he doubted he'd ever taste again. After his parents had died, it was discovered that the embargo and the war had destroyed their business. There was no money left, and strangers now lived in his Boston home.

"Come on," he said, jumping to his feet. "We're certainly not doing much good up here."

"You're right," Lucy agreed as she stood and brushed dirt and leaves from her skirt, "but it's good to get away for a few moments. Even if the view does look down on a dried-up river."

They walked quietly down from the bluff together, crossing the small bridge over Deer Creek. Ben walked Lucy back to her house before returning to Richard's small cabin at the edge of the woods. He filled the water bucket at the well and, heaving with all his might, carried the sloshing bucket into the kitchen for Susannah. Soon his muscles would be as strong as Richard's.

Susannah smiled and thanked him, and little Tim came running to greet him.

"Uncle Ben," he said. "Look." He held up a whistle that Ben had carved for him, which was now in two pieces. "Pamela broke it," he declared. "She's a bad girl."

Pamela clung to her mother's skirts, sucking two fingers of her free hand. When she heard her brother's accusations, she ducked her head.

Ben took the pieces of the whistle. "She didn't mean to break it," he said. "And I can easily make another."

Timothy began to bounce around. "Would you, Uncle Ben? Please, would you?"

"We'll look for a just-right willow branch tomorrow."

Just then, Richard appeared at the door. "Tomorrow you may be busy, little brother," he said. "Come out to the well. I want to teach you to dress out the game. Bring that sharp knife of yours."

Ben gave a little shudder as he thought of the blood and innards he was about to see. But he straightened himself, pulled his knife from his trouser pocket, and followed Richard out into the dooryard. A flickering lantern sat on the edge of the well, spreading light on the ground where Richard had placed two dead rabbits.

"Just do as I do," Richard said, lifting one of the rabbits by its hind legs. Taking his knife, he carefully made a clean slit down the midsection of the rabbit.

Ben took a quick breath and held it. Giving himself no time to think, he did the same. Within minutes two rabbits were skinned and gutted. Ben was pretty proud of himself, and once it was over and the entrails were lying on the ground, it didn't seem half bad. Like Lucy said, he could get over being afraid.

Without the fur, the rabbits looked pretty skinny. As though reading Ben's thoughts, Richard said, "They've about run all their winter fat off." Taking water from the dipper hanging on the well post, he rinsed both carcasses. "But wild game may be all that will grace our table until things change."

Ben wanted to ask questions, but he held his peace.

Heading toward the house, Richard gave one more comment. "And the game is staying farther and farther away from all this so-called civilization."

That night's supper was salt pork and Indian corn pone, but Susannah seemed delighted that she now had two rabbits to stew.

The next morning Richard woke Ben early. Ben quickly dressed and ate, then helped Susannah pack their lunch of dried beef, biscuits, and water. Benjamin followed close behind Richard as they made their way across Deer Creek and headed in a northeasterly direction until they were far from the noisy city.

Ben had never been in such dense wilderness, but he rather liked the solitude. Silently, Richard pointed out tracks and signs of game.

Before the day was out, Richard placed his prized musket in Ben's hands and showed him how to pour in the correct amount of powder and tamp it in. Then he demonstrated wrapping the lead ball with the cloth and tamping it down.

"This is the safety cock," Richard said, placing the percussion cap in place. "When you're ready to fire, you pull it back to full cock, then let her fly."

Ben nodded, wondering if he would falter when it came time to fire.

"Someday," Richard said softly, "I'm gonna have me a good rifle."

A few moments later, Richard pointed out a fat grouse sitting crouched beneath a bramble bush. As Ben drew a bead on the bird, his hands began to quiver and shake. He forced them to be still. Slowly he let the hammer fly, and the explosion slammed his shoulder. The grouse flew away unharmed.

He waited for Richard to berate him, but his brother only remarked, "Being hungry can help make you a crack shot."

It was true. When they stopped to drink from a stream and eat their lunch, all Ben could think of was rabbit stew! After that, he pictured food on the table every time he aimed. Late in the afternoon, he had a bead on a squirrel sitting high in a beech tree. Slowly, slowly he let the hammer fly, and the squirrel fell to the ground with a thud.

Ben wanted to laugh and shout, but instead he handed the musket to Richard and ran to pick up his kill. When he came back, Richard patted his shoulder and said, "Good shot. You must be real hungry!" As they laughed together, Ben wondered why he and his brother couldn't have more moments like this.

A few days later, Ben and Lucy were sent to the market to see what they could purchase. In just a few weeks the open markets in Cincinnati had totally changed. The grapes, melons, and tomatoes that Lucy had promised would not be coming. No milk, cheese, or fat hens. The drought had affected the crops. Most of what little the farmers produced they were using themselves. And what was brought into market often went begging because so few people had money to make purchases.

In spite of the early hour, the air was still and hot. Under the roof of the vast market, there were only a smattering of wagons. And the produce looked pitiful. Ben was almost embarrassed to approach the farmers. Lucy did a little dickering and purchased a bag of snap beans, two small heads of cabbage, and a few eggs. Before they turned for home, Ben suggested they go to Lidell's.

"But we've no money for candy," she protested.

"I know, but I'd like to say hello to John."

Lucy looked at him. "Do you think he still has a job there?"

Ben shrugged. "Let's find out."

"Let's do. If he's there, I can find out how Charlotte is as well."

They hurried in the direction of Fourth Street. Inside the store there was only one other customer. Charles hailed them as they entered. "Say there, Lucy, Ben," he said with a cheery smile. "Did you come to buy me out?"

Lucy chuckled at his silly remark. "I don't think we're in a position to buy you out today, Charles. We're looking for John. Does he still work for you?"

"Well," Charles said slowly, "he doesn't exactly work for me. I guess you could say he works with me now."

"What do you mean?" Ben asked.

Charles leaned against the counter and gave a little sigh. "When the crash hit, I had to let my workers go."

"I know how that is," Lucy put in. "Papa and George had to do the same at the boatworks."

Charles rubbed at the scar on his face and nodded. "It's the same everywhere. In Pittsburgh and Lexington, too, I hear. Well, anyway, that John just wouldn't go." He chuckled as he thought about it. "John says, 'You can't pay me, but you can teach me. Let me stay and do what I can, and you teach me all about the mercantile business.' "

57

Ben nodded. He knew he liked John Hendricks. That boy was smart.

"So," Charles went on, "he comes every day. We wait on a few customers, and then I teach him how to make orders, how to stock, and how to keep the books." He laughed again. "Course there're no orders to make, so we pretend a great deal."

"So where's John now?" Lucy asked. Ben was just ready to ask the same thing.

The light in Charles's eyes faded just a bit. "Today John is at home helping his family move."

"Move?" Lucy asked. "Are they moving away from Cincinnati?"

"Oh no, Little Lucy, they're just moving to another part of town. You see, they've lost their house."

Ben felt his stomach lurch and he heard Lucy gasp. "Oh no," she said. "Poor Charlotte. Poor Mr. and Mrs. Hendricks." Ben knew that Lucy had been frightened they might lose their house after she learned that Mr. and Mrs. Martin Baum, the richest people in Cincinnati, had lost all their holdings.

"Lots of people are losing houses and land right along with their businesses," Charles told them. "That's what happens when people live on credit. Me, I've tried to pay for everything as I go. My ma and pa taught me that long before they died." He shook his head. "But even still, we may not make it through this."

"Where'd the Hendricks move to?" Ben wanted to know.

"They found a small cabin over by Mill Creek."

"That's clear out of town." Lucy was incredulous.

"Yep," Charles answered, "and they were plenty lucky to get it."

Before Lucy and Ben left, Charles held out the candy jar. "Here," he said, "each of you take one. They're getting staler by the day." He smiled. "I promise I won't tell if you won't."

Ben hated to take something without paying and he could see Lucy felt the same way. But Charles insisted.

Soon they were carrying their basket between them, walking down the hill, sucking on the spicy peppermint sticks.

"What are you thinking about, Ben?" Lucy asked as she licked the last of the peppermint from her fingers.

They had just passed the corner where Raggy had accosted them so long ago. Ben hadn't seen Raggy for weeks. "I was just thinking," Ben answered. "If things keep going as they are, Raggy Wallace may become the best-dressed fellow in Cincinnati."

CHAPTER 8
Surprise in the Country

The Fourth of July, usually a rollicking celebration in Cincinnati, was quiet and subdued that summer. The city council voted to dispense with the great parade and instead encouraged citizens to become involved in the soup kitchens that had been set up in each part of the city. There were a few fireworks displays that evening, but they didn't amount to much.

Lucy was disappointed. She'd looked forward to the holiday as a diversion from the gloom about her. Still, she knew the city leaders were right. How could they celebrate when people were starving?

However, a nice surprise did come a few days later. In the mail came a letter from Betsy and Andrew Farley. The

Farleys were relatives of theirs who lived on a farm several miles north of the city. Lucy wanted to open the letter right away, but Mama said they must wait until Papa came home.

It was later than usual when Papa arrived home that night. Lucy wanted to show him the letter right away, but Mama said to wait. "Let Papa eat supper and rest his weary bones," she said. Even though Mama was tired from all the daily household chores, still she took extra care to protect Papa and make him comfortable each evening.

Finally after their meager supper was finished, Lucy brought the letter to the table. "Look, Papa. A letter from Betsy and Andrew. May I help open it?"

Papa smiled. "Of course you can, Little Lucy. Let's hope it's full of good news. I could use some."

Carefully Lucy peeled open the seal and spread out the paper. She read: " 'Dear Paul, Ellie, and Little Lucy. . .' " Lucy looked up. "When is everyone going to stop calling me Little Lucy?" she asked.

"Go on," Mama insisted. "What does Betsy say?"

Lucy read on:

"We've heard about the hard times in the city. The drought here has been bad as well, but we do have plenty to eat. Andrew has dug the foundation for the new room on the house. We could use help in framing and finishing it.

"Why don't you come for a visit and lend a hand? Have George and Patricia come, too. It would be good to see you again. Tell Lucy I have a surprise for her to see.

Love,
Betsy

Lucy looked up to see Mama smiling. "A trip to the farm," Mama said softly. "That would be nice."

"And listen to this part," Lucy said. "At the bottom it says, 'Our baby is to arrive around Thanksgiving time.'"

"Oh Paul, do you hear that? Betsy is to have her first baby. What wonderful news."

"May we go, Papa? They need our help. You heard what she said. May we?" A surprise. Betsy had said there was a surprise. Lucy wondered what it could be.

"She did say they need help," Papa agreed. He leaned back in his chair. "I guess nothing here will spoil while we're gone."

Lucy could hardly contain her excitement. How good it would be to have something to look forward to once again. "Papa," she said, "may we take Ben along?"

When her father paused before answering, she added, "He can work hard. Why, he's even learned to swing an axe."

"Doesn't Susannah need him there, Lucy?" Mama asked.

"As Ben himself said," Lucy answered. "He's just another mouth to feed. They barely have enough to eat now."

Mama and Papa looked at one another. Finally, Papa said, "Let's ask Richard. If he agrees, it's all right with me."

Lucy jumped up from where she was sitting. "Please, Papa. May we take the lantern and go to Richard's house tonight?"

"Lucy," Mama protested. "Your papa is weary. Let him rest."

"It's all right, Eleanor. Richard's gone out hunting nearly every day. I'd just as well go while he's at home." He stood up from the table. "Leave the dishes and grab your bonnet and come with us," he said to Mama.

She nodded. "It would be good to spend a little time with

Susannah," she said. "Paul, would you go to the cellar and bring salt pork from our barrel? We shouldn't go empty-handed."

Lucy was already running upstairs to grab her bonnet from off the hook in her room. She and Ben were going to go to the farm! Richard just had to say yes.

And Richard did say yes. His only condition was for Ben to cut extra wood for Susannah's cookstove before he left.

Richard had carried a couple of cane chairs out to the back stoop where he and Papa sat in the warm night air talking softly. Inside Mama played with little Pam while she chatted with Susannah. Lucy and Ben ran about the clearing, helping Timothy catch fireflies.

Stretched on boards at the edge of the clearing were the skins that Richard was tanning.

"This is the one I shot," Ben said, pointing to the golden-brown squirrel hide. "Richard says he'll teach me to make a pair of moccasins with it. And in the fall, if I shoot a deer, he'll teach me to make leggings."

Lucy noted the pride in his voice. Perhaps Ben was finally adjusting to his new home.

The next day, Papa began making arrangements for their trip. To rent a wagon for the trip, he had to write a promise to the livery man that he would bring back produce from the farm in payment.

The morning they were to leave, Ben was at their house before daybreak. Mama made sure he ate another biscuit before they left. In a basket sitting by the front door, Mama had packed a lunch to eat on the way.

George and Papa had walked to the livery to fetch the wagon, and Lucy sat on the front steps waiting. Her insides were a jumble of fluttering butterflies. It had been months since they'd been out to visit the Farley farm.

She kept wondering about the word "surprise." Betsy had written in the letter that a baby was on the way, so that wasn't it. With a slam of the door, Ben came out carrying a buttered biscuit.

"Thank you for asking me to go along, Lucy," he said.

Lucy wondered if she remembered to say thank you half as many times as Ben did. "I wanted you to go see the farm. It's ever so much fun."

"What's it like?"

"Fields of grain that seem to stretch out for forever," she explained. "And a barn full of hay with cows, horses, pigs. Oh, and there are geese, too."

"Are the geese mean?"

Lucy laughed. "They're just like the pigs on the street, Ben. You take a big stick to them."

Just then around the corner came Papa and George with the wagon. Harnesses jingled, and the team of sorrel horses whinnied and snuffled and bobbed their heads as Papa pulled them to a stop. "Whoa there," he called out.

"Mercy to goodness," Mama said as she came out carrying the basket. "That's enough commotion to wake all the neighbors."

Mama was probably right. Lucy was quite sure no one else in the neighborhood was up this early. The buckboard had two sets of seats up front with a long bed in back and high sideboards. George hopped down to help Patricia up into the back seat. Lucy and Ben clamored into the wagon bed. Once Mama and Papa were onboard, they were off.

They took Hamilton Road north out of the city. In no time at all, they were traveling along a curving road that cut through dense stands of trees. Occasionally they came upon open farmland where acres of wheat, oats, barley, and corn had been planted. Cozy little houses snuggled into hillsides flanked by smaller smokehouses, outhouses, sheds, and at least one towering barn.

Lucy had heard many times what fertile farmland their state enjoyed. And it was true. But Papa commented on the scrawny crops. "They should be a full foot taller by this time of year."

Mama replied that they should all be praying for rain.

Lucy breathed in the clean, fresh air and grinned at Ben. She didn't want to think about droughts, about bank failures, or about financial disasters. This was a holiday, and she was determined to enjoy it to the fullest.

"I hope there are baby kittens in the barn," she said.

"I like kittens," Ben said. "I had a kitten of my own in Boston."

"Your very own?"

Ben nodded. "She even stayed with me in my room."

Lucy thought that would be nice. A cuddly little kitten lying on her bed. "Say," she said, "maybe that's the surprise."

"What surprise?" Ben asked.

"In Betsy's letter she said there was a surprise for me to see. Maybe it's a kitten."

Over her shoulder, Mama said, "Lucy, if the surprise is a kitten, you cannot bring it home."

Lucy thought a moment. "And since I've seen kittens before, the surprise must not be a kitten."

When the warm sun was straight up in the sky, Papa stopped at a stream and allowed the horses to drink. Lucy and Ben hopped down and helped spread the quilts in the grass. They opened the basket and enjoyed a picnic lunch of salt pork, slices of bread with cheese, and boiled eggs. No one commented that it wasn't a very elegant picnic lunch. It was too lovely a spot and too nice a day to complain.

Papa brought a dipper of water for the ladies, but Lucy and Ben knelt down at the edge of the gurgling stream and scooped up handsful of clear, cool water. "It's a far sight cleaner than Deer Creek," Lucy said.

Just then, Ben flicked cold water on her.

"Why you!" She scooped up a cupped palm and flung it at him, splashing him square in the face.

Ben burst out laughing and ran from her reach as she chased him through the trees. She very nearly caught him, but since he'd been spending time in the woods with Richard, he was much more agile than when she'd first met him. For the life of her, she couldn't keep up with him.

Papa's call put a stop to their game, and they came laughing and panting to the wagon. Later, Lucy realized that it was the first time she'd ever heard Ben laugh. Really laugh!

As dusk began to gather, the rocking of the wagon lulled Lucy into a deep slumber. The next thing she knew loud voices called out: "Hello, hello. Welcome. We thought you'd never get here. Come on down. Let Andrew take care of the team. I know you're tired."

Even in her half-sleep, Lucy recognized Betsy's friendly voice. Rubbing her eyes, she sat up. Ben was still fast asleep on his pile of quilts. She reached over and gave him a shake. "Sleepyhead. Wake up. We're here."

Lanterns were swinging over the back of the wagon. "Well, well. If it's not our Little Lucy."

That was Andrew's voice. "And who's this?" he wanted to know.

Ben was sitting up and stretching.

"This is Ben," Lucy said. "Richard's younger brother."

"Of course, of course. Come on, now," he said, giving them each a hand. "Betsy has a supper all laid out."

Following soft yellow lantern light, the two went up the path to the back door. Tantalizing food aromas met them before they entered. Lucy was sure nothing had ever smelled so good. There on the table were platters of frizzled ham, bowls of seasoned potatoes, and wedges of cooked cabbage. But on the sideboard was the best of all—squash pies. Lucy hadn't seen a pie for ever so long.

Lucy and Ben ate without talking. Lucy wasn't sure if it was because she was too tired to talk or too hungry. But as she cut into her thick slice of golden squash pie, she remembered about the surprise.

"Betsy," she blurted out. "You said there was a surprise for me to see."

"And there is. There surely is," Betsy said.

"May I see it?"

"It's in the barn," Betsy explained.

"May we take the lantern out to the barn and see?"

"No surprises tonight, Little Lucy," Mama said firmly. "To bed with you as soon as you finish eating."

Once Lucy and Ben were bedded down on quilts in corners of the kitchen, she was glad Mama had said no. Her full stomach had now made her very sleepy. As she dozed off, Lucy knew it wouldn't matter if there were no surprise at all. Just being at the farm was a good enough treat!

CHAPTER 9
Ben's Gifts

Early the next morning, Lucy was awakened by the sounds of Betsy filling the cookstove with wood. When she looked over to wake Ben, he was gone. How could he be up before her?

"Betsy!" she said, jumping to her feet. "Where's Ben?"

"He volunteered to chop kindling for the stove." Tall, willowy Betsy leaned down to grab another chunk of wood, shoved it in the stove, and slammed the iron door shut. Corn mush bubbled in a pot, and tall round biscuits sat on a tin ready to go into the oven. Outside a noisy old rooster hailed the morning with loud crowing. How could Lucy have slept through all this noise?

As she hurriedly folded quilts, she asked, "He hasn't been to the barn, has he?"

Betsy laughed. "Do you think I'd let someone else see the secret first?"

Lucy felt a stab of guilt. That's exactly what she'd thought. Just then Mama came in from the living room. Lucy ran to give her mother a hug. Mama's face seemed free of worry lines for the first time in many days. "Mama, may I run to the barn before breakfast?"

Mama shook her head. "Breakfast first, Little Lucy."

Lucy wanted to complain, but seeing Mama so relaxed made her keep still. She wanted nothing to ruin this perfect day.

The men were outside studying the foundation for the new room and planning the day's work. Quickly Mama, Patricia, and Lucy helped Betsy put breakfast on, then they called everyone inside. Lucy saw Ben's eyes brighten at the grand array of food on the table. Since there weren't enough chairs, Ben and Lucy filled their plates and ate on the back stoop.

Chickens scratched about the yard. Several tall white geese strutted proudly, giving out an occasional honk. The smell of the clean country air invigorated Lucy and made her want to run and shout.

"I don't know which is best," Lucy told Ben, "the sweet, clean air or the scrumptious food."

Around a mouthful of biscuit, Ben mumbled, "Both."

Lucy laughed as this boy with the impeccable manners sopped gravy with his biscuit and swiped a drip off his chin with his sleeve. When his plate was clean, Ben said, "Betsy told me this morning that she's been carrying water from the well to her garden each day."

"Looks like it needs it."

"We could do that."

Lucy stopped with a spoonful of mush in the air. "That's a kindly thought. Between us we can carry twice as much water as Betsy in her condition." Cleaning up the last of her bowl of mush, she jumped to her feet. "Come on, there's so much to do. And we have a surprise to see."

"Don't tell me to come on," Ben teased. "You're the one who slept all morning."

"Slept all morning? Why Benjamin Allerton. You. . ." She smacked at him with her spoon, but he ducked quickly into the kitchen.

When breakfast dishes were cleared, Betsy finally announced that it was time to go to the barn. Ben and Lucy ran circles around Betsy, laughing and giggling, as they followed the dusty path from the house to the barn. Chickens squawked and scattered from in front of the trio. Rhythmic sounds of hammering and sawing filled the air as the men framed in the new room.

Betsy chatted about how pleased she was that they'd come and how excited she was about the new bedroom. When they reached the barn, Ben helped her pull open the heavy door. Lucy squinted at the dimness and inhaled the smells of leather, fresh hay, and animal dung. Andrew's prize horses were stabled in the barn, but most of the cows and pigs were outside in the pasture.

After a moment, Lucy heard a faint baa-ing sound. "Sheep?" she asked, making a guess.

"Over here," Betsy said, leading to a far corner. There in a small enclosure were a couple nanny goats and three of the most darling white kids Betsy had ever seen.

"Goats!" she exclaimed. "You have goats. Oh Betsy, this is a wonderful surprise. Where did they come from? May we pet them?" She wanted to touch their silky fur.

Betsy reached up to get a bucket from a hook and then fetched a small stool. "An old peddler came by awhile back with these nanny goats, and Andrew and I took one look and we couldn't resist. We just had to have them. Then a few weeks later they gave birth to these three kids."

As Betsy opened the gate to the enclosure, the nearest nanny moved cautiously away. "Come now, Milly," Betsy cooed to the nanny. "They're not sure they trust me just yet. So you two just watch until I finish milking."

"Milking? You're going to milk them?" Lucy was fascinated. Such small animals giving milk. She watched carefully as Betsy fastened the nanny's head in a stanchion to keep her still. Streams of milk made a pinging sound as they hit the tin bucket. Soon the white foam rose to the rim where Lucy could see it.

"These little critters give a lot of milk," Betsy told them. She handed the full bucket to Ben. "Set that over by the door so it won't get spilled, and I'll let her loose now."

Betsy unfastened the stanchion and then repeated the process with Milliken, the other nanny. Once she was done, she opened the gate to let Ben and Lucy in. "Walk slowly so as not to startle them."

Lucy knelt down in the hay to pet one of the kids. The coat was warm and silky to her touch. She rubbed its head and the kid pushed back. "Look Betsy. Look how she's trying to butt."

"You're right, that is a she. A little nanny," Betsy said. "You should see them butting one another. Like three little children romping together. Cutest thing you ever saw."

71

"Are these ones nannies, too?" Ben asked, his arm about the necks of the other two kids.

"On your right is a billy goat, a male," Betsy replied. "The other one is a nanny."

"Will they run and play with us?" Lucy wanted to know.

Betsy nodded. "They'll give you a merry chase. You'll have to keep a close eye on them."

"Let's work for a while," Ben suggested to Lucy, "then we'll come back and play with them later this afternoon."

"That's a perfect idea."

"Work? And what work will you be doing?" Betsy led the way out and closed the small gate to the enclosure.

Ben looked at Lucy as though waiting for her to speak. But she said, "You tell her. It was your idea."

His face flushed pink as he said, "We'd like to carry water to your garden while we're here."

"Why, Ben, thank you." Betsy leaned over to put her arm around him and kissed him squarely on the cheek. Now his face grew even more red. "What a relief it'll be to have a rest."

Time passed quickly as Ben and Lucy carried heavy buckets of water to the rows of vegetables. The hot sun bore down on their heads. Lucy found wearing her bonnet was much more comfortable than having it hanging down her back. Andrew gave Ben a felt slouch hat to wear to shade his face.

They hoed weeds in the corn patch, then picked a basket of snap beans. Mama and Patricia picked cucumbers and cooked up vinegar syrup to make pickles. There were carrots, turnips, and cabbages ready to be picked. Along the fence grew vines of ripening melons and pumpkins. Lucy wished she lived on a farm with all this food growing everywhere.

The open-air market didn't seem half so much fun. Before supper, Ben and Lucy released the goats and played tirelessly about the farmyard.

The next day, Ben found several pieces of scrap lumber lying about where the men were working. Taking them to Betsy, he said, "I noticed you have no whatnot shelf in the house. I can make one from these pieces. Would you like that?"

"Benjamin, you'll never know how much I'd like that. Andrew is able to put up a barn and drive a nail straight, but fancy work is not his cup of tea."

Ben had his trusty knife, and in the evenings, while Lucy ran about playing with baby goats, Ben carved a delicately detailed whatnot shelf.

The days were passing too swiftly for Lucy. She wanted this holiday to last forever. But within a week, the room was framed and finished, and there were even two glass windows hung. In the living room, Betsy's new whatnot shelf was mounted in the corner by the fireplace. Even Andrew commented on what a craftsman Benjamin was.

The women packed foodstuffs to take home. Some would pay the livery man, but there was still plenty to share with Richard and Susannah. There were green pickles, blackberry preserves, blocks of cheese, and baskets of goose and chicken eggs. One bag of wheat and another of corn lay in the wagon bed.

On the last afternoon, Lucy and Ben sat under a leafy buckeye tree with the nannies and their kids munching grass nearby.

"Betsy says goats grow up and come fresh much quicker than a cow," Lucy said.

"Come fresh?"

"Give milk."

Ben nodded. "Oh."

"And she says they eat very little, and that they'll eat most anything. They don't need a big pasture like a cow."

"I heard Betsy say that." Ben was lying on his back staring up at the cloudless sky.

"Ben, you know how we're always wishing we could do more to help out our families?"

"We do what we can. Now that I can shoot the musket and skin my own game, I feel I'm pulling my share of the load."

"What if we could do more?"

"More? How?" Ben sat up and looked at Lucy. "I can tell you're thinking about something. What are you cooking up?"

"What if we could sell goat's milk?"

"It'd spoil before we got it back to Cincinnati," Ben said.

"What if we took the milk-giver with us?"

Ben smiled. "You want to take one of the nannies?"

"Yes, I want to take Milliken." Lucy smiled. "Her kid is weaned from her."

"Your mama would never allow a goat in your yard."

"A few months ago she might not. But now that there's little food and no money, she might not be so hard to convince."

Ben thought about it. "It'd be fun to have Milliken with us," he said.

"I agree. Shall we go ask?"

"Let's go!"

First they went to find Betsy, who was out in the garden. Lucy asked if she'd part with Milliken. "I was hoping you'd ask," Betsy answered.

Mama and Patricia were in the kitchen cutting up a roasting hen for supper.

As Lucy expected, her mother protested. "Little Lucy,"

she said, "you don't know a thing about taking care of a goat. You're too young for that much responsibility."

"I'm not too young," Lucy protested. "I can learn. We'll have milk to drink and some left over to sell."

"But you don't know how to milk a goat."

"Betsy's already taught me. There's nothing to it."

Just then, Ben spoke up. "I can build a pen and a stanchion, Aunt Ellie."

Now Mama hesitated. It was a good sign.

Then Ben added, "And I'll even help Lucy take care of Milliken."

Lucy could see her mother weakening. "I suppose we could see what your papa thinks."

Papa thought it was the smartest idea he'd heard in a long time. "Fresh milk every day," he quipped. "Why, Eleanor, who could argue with that?"

So it was settled. Andrew wove a tether rope for them with a handy slipknot so Milliken wouldn't get away from them. The next morning when they packed the wagon, the men tied Milliken to the back.

Lucy had thought she would be sad about returning to the city, but now that she had Milliken, she was excited. Loud good-byes and thank-you's were exchanged as the wagon pulled out of the Farley farmyard. The return trip would be slower since the wagon was weighted down with supplies.

Milliken wasn't sure she liked leaving the farm. She bleated most of the way. Mama put her hands over her ears. "Such a racket. Sounds worse than a colicky baby."

Papa answered, "You won't care about the noise when she gives buckets of milk."

Lucy didn't mind the noise at all. What fun she was going to have with her new pet.

CHAPTER 10
Milliken's Accident

The next morning, Lucy and Ben were ready to launch into their milk-selling business. But while they had plenty of milk to sell, they'd forgotten one small detail. Few people had the money with which to make a purchase.

Ben had a small wagon in which to carry their crocks of milk. They walked from house to house, pulling the wagon and asking if anyone wanted to buy milk. People sadly shook their heads and closed their doors. Lucy and Ben went home discouraged.

It was Ben who came up with the idea of bartering. "No one has any money," he said, "but people have things they might want to trade."

"That's a wonderful idea," Lucy agreed.

"Let's begin with Lidell's store," Ben suggested. "We'll ask Susannah and Aunt Ellie what they need from the store, then we'll ask Charles Lidell if he'll trade the items for goat's milk."

And that's just what they did. Charles Lidell was delighted with the plan because he and his wife had two small children. At last, Lucy felt she was truly being a help to her family.

When Papa learned of their plan, he commended them. To Mama he said, "Little Lucy and Ben make a fine business team."

Lucy basked in his praise, but she still wished he'd stop calling her Little Lucy.

Milliken's tether rope was seldom used. Lucy could go nowhere but what the bleating nanny wasn't right on her heels. Lucy used the rope only when she took Milliken into town.

"That silly goat would sleep with you if she could," Mama said in exasperation.

And Lucy wished Milliken could sleep with her. The enclosure Ben built was situated in a corner of the small area behind the house, but Milliken spent little time there. Not because the pen wasn't sufficient, but because the goat cried when no one was around. Lucy had never before had a pet, and Milliken's antics made her laugh with glee.

And laughter was sorely needed, for as the hot, dry summer wore on, conditions in the city worsened. Food supplies dwindled and people went hungry. There weren't as many hogs roaming the streets these days. Papa heard that people were catching them and eating them. Lucy knew butchering a large animal in the heat of summer meant meat that rotted quickly. People became very ill eating spoiled meat. Knowing this made her even more thankful for the small store of food they now had in the cellar.

Papa and George talked about another trip to the country. They planned to help other farmers with building projects in trade for food. Lucy thought it was a good plan and was pleased that her Papa thought of it.

For the most part, Lucy had shoved the thought of her new piano far into the back of her mind. It seemed selfish to want a luxury such as a piano when people were hungry.

However, one day as she and Ben were on an errand for Mama, with Milliken on her tether rope, Lucy was again thinking about her longing for a piano.

They were coming back from Lidell's store when Lucy had a bright idea. "No one's in the church on a Tuesday," she said to Ben. "Let's stop in for a minute."

"Lucy, you don't like the long hours at church on Sunday. Why do you want to go on a Tuesday?"

Lucy studied Ben. His unruly mop of cornsilk-colored hair stuck out every which way beneath his cap. The cutdown trousers were already too short for him. Susannah had once said that Ben grew at least an inch a day. Where he used to be pale and wan, he was now ruddy and sunburned. Ben looked nothing like the dapper boy who came to them from Boston.

"I do so like church. . .at least part of church," she retorted.

"Only the music."

"Nothing wrong with that. Music holds a sermon in itself." Tugging on Milliken's rope, she called out, "Are you coming with me or not?" The nanny, who was attempting to nibble tufts of dried grass growing at the edge of the street, bleated and gave a little leap as she scurried to follow along.

"Lucy, what're you going to do?"

"The way things look, I may never have a piano of my own."

"You're not going inside the church?"

"People go into the church all the time to pray. Why can't I?"

As Ben came up beside Lucy, Milliken gave him a playful butt in the leg. He reached down to scratch her head. "That's not exactly true," he said to Lucy. "You're not going to pray, are you?"

She smiled. "I can pray while I'm looking at the piano, can't I?"

"Lucy!"

"I just want to lift the cover and touch the keys. There's no reason why I can't touch it. It's not fair for Widow Tuthill to be the only one allowed to play it."

"You'll have your piano someday, Lucy, I just know it. Susannah always says to me, 'Let patience have her perfect work.' "

"I know. Mama quotes the same verse to me all the time. And I am being patient. Very patient. But while I'm being patient, I can still look at the church piano."

They came down Walnut Street to where the stone church with its towering bell steeple loomed on a corner lot.

"What will you do with Milliken?" Ben asked.

"You hold her and stand outside to keep watch. We'll go to the side door. There's a little grass under the tree there. Milliken will like that."

The shade cast by the church felt good to Lucy's hot feet. Here the blazing summer sun had not totally scorched the scrubby grass. "Stay on the steps," she instructed Ben. "If you see someone coming, rap hard on the door." She handed Milliken's rope to him.

Reaching out to take it, Ben said, "I shouldn't help you get in trouble, you know."

"There'll be no trouble, Ben." She stepped up on the cool stone step. Glancing about, she saw no one. The brass knob turned easily in her hand. "I'll leave the door ajar. Remember, rap hard."

Ben nodded, then sat down on the step and let Milliken's rope out to give her wide range of the available grass.

Inside the church the air was cool, with a kind of musty aroma. Lucy made her way past the rows of pews to where the lovely piano sat. Soft light from the window fell across the shiny wood, making it gleam. With trembling fingers, she reached for the little knobs on the front and lifted the cover. It folded back once, then lifted once more to expose all the neatly lined black and white keys. Nervously, she glanced over her shoulder. The sanctuary was still empty and quiet.

Her heart was fairly thudding in her throat. She spread her skirt and sat primly on the stool, then allowed herself to actually reach out and touch the keys. They were as cool and glossy as she knew they would be. Without pressing a key, she trailed her fingers up and down the keyboard. In her mind, she saw how Widow Tuthill's fingers pounded out the chords for the hymns every Sunday. She wondered if there were a lighter way to make the melodies come to life.

From the music rack, she pulled down the hymnal and fanned through the pages. If only she knew how to read the notes. Surely it wouldn't hurt to press just one key. She did, and the sound of the note startled her. She pressed another and then another. Within a few moments, she found sets of notes that sounded pleasing together and others that grated on her ears.

A little noise sounded behind her, making her gasp.

Turning around, she said, "Oh, Milliken. It's only you."

Then she jumped from where she was sitting. From the nanny's mouth hung a partially chewed hymnal. Down the aisle were three more that also were partially chewed.

"Milliken! What are you doing in here?"

"And I might ask you the same thing, young lady!" There at the door stood Widow Tuthill.

Lucy froze. Where was Ben? Why hadn't he rapped on the door?

Widow Tuthill snapped her parasol shut and tucked it beneath her arm. With a scowl on her thin face, she walked slowly up the aisle. Her long black silk dress made little swishing noises as she picked up bits and pieces of chewed hymnals along the way.

"Just wait until I talk to your parents about this," she said sternly, her eyes narrowing. "Not only have you broken the rules about not touching my piano, but you have allowed this mangy animal inside the house of God."

Lucy stood to her full height. "Milliken isn't mangy. And she didn't mean any harm. I didn't bring her in, she. . ." Lucy stopped. She'd better not say that she'd left Ben to guard the door. Where could he be? She knelt down to take the hymnal from Milliken and placed it on a pew. The edges were a mess. Milliken bleated and gave Lucy a gentle butt in the arm.

The widow stepped to the piano, took out her lace hankie, carefully wiped down the keys, then quietly closed the lid. "You are never to touch this piano. Is that clear?"

"Yes, ma'am." Lucy twisted the ends of Milliken's dangling rope.

"Now take that creature and leave the premises. I'll discuss this with the Reverend Corwin and then we'll pay a visit to your parents and discuss your actions."

"Yes, ma'am," Lucy said again. She tugged at the rope and started down the aisle, then stopped. "I'm very sorry about the damage Milliken caused. But I think more people should be allowed to use the piano," she said boldly. "After all, the church belongs to everyone."

Widow Tuthill pressed the hankie to her forehead, then made scooting motions with her hand. "Go. Leave, before my anger takes over."

Out in the hot sunshine, Lucy looked up and down the street for Ben. Nothing. Something had to have happened. But what?

All she knew to do was to head toward home. No sooner had she left Walnut to turn onto Second Street, then Ben came running toward her from a side street.

"Hey, Lucy! I almost caught him," he called out.

"Benjamin Allerton. How could you? I left you to guard the door and you deserted your post." She stopped and waited for him to catch up. Perspiration dripped from his beet-red face. His hat was scrunched in his hand, and he was heaving great breaths. Suddenly his words registered. "Almost caught who?" Lucy wanted to know.

"Why, Raggy. Who else?"

"You were chasing Raggy Wallace?"

Ben beamed a wide smile. "I did."

"Why? What did he do?"

"He tried to come at me and grab Milliken's rope. So I stood up to him and gave him a hard shove."

Lucy could barely believe her ears. "Then what?"

"He tried to fight back, and I tripped him. When he started to run, I tied Milliken to the doorknob and chased him. Almost caught him, too."

Lucy shook her head. This was almost worth getting

caught by Widow Tuthill. She had touched the piano, and Ben had chased Raggy. Two splendid victories!

When she told Ben about Milliken getting loose and what happened to the hymnals and about the widow coming in, he was crestfallen. "I'm sorry. Your papa will be angry with you. What do you think will happen?"

"If Raggy tried to steal Milliken, you did the right thing. Whatever happens will happen."

Mama was embarrassed and quite distraught following the visit from the Reverend Corwin. Papa didn't seem quite as upset as Mama, but Lucy was duly scolded by both and sent to bed early that night. Mama and Papa agreed that somehow Lucy would have to pay for the hymnals, no matter how long it took.

"Perhaps I can find people who will pay cash for Milliken's milk," Lucy said solemnly. "Then I'll be able to pay the debt." But the thought made Lucy feel badly since she'd hoped to use the milk to help Mama and Papa.

Sitting on the edge of her small rope bed, she gazed out the window, wishing she were outside playing. Evenings in the summer were the best times for playing because it was cooler. Only a slight breeze ruffled the treetops, and it was stuffy and hot in her bedroom.

The thought of Ben chasing Raggy through the streets amazed Lucy. When she had asked him what he would have done if he'd caught him, Ben had said he didn't know. With Raggy's larger size, he could whip Ben. But Ben had saved Milliken. If Raggy had stolen the nanny, he'd probably be having her for supper right about now.

Lucy was sorry the hymnals had been chewed up, because she loved the fine songbooks their church owned. But she'd never be sorry she touched those lovely ivory keys. Closing her eyes, she made herself remember how they felt beneath her fingers. "Let patience have her perfect work." Waiting was so hard, how could it be a "perfect" work?

CHAPTER 11
The Storm

Because of Milliken's size, Lucy had a hard time leading her around. If Ben weren't with Lucy, Milliken nearly dragged Lucy by the tether. But when left in her enclosure, the goat set up such a racket that the neighbors complained. Lucy lived on a crowded street where houses were close together. The offer of goat's milk did nothing to appease the disgruntled neighbors.

"We need our sleep," said Mr. McGibbons, who lived directly behind them. Mrs. McGibbons, who had five little ones, heartily agreed.

There was nothing to do but let Ben take Milliken to his house. In the clearing near the banks of Deer Creek, there were fewer houses nearby. Ben dismantled the enclosure and used the rough planks of lumber to construct a new one behind the Allerton home.

Even though she knew it was for the best, Lucy was sad to have to part with Milliken. Of course, she'd see the goat often, but it wasn't the same as having her right outside the back door.

Both Timmy and Pam were delighted to have Milliken at their house and squealed with delight when she licked their hands.

Being nearer the woods turned out to be much better for Milliken. She could be tethered among the trees far from the house, where she could eat grass and weeds to her heart's content.

It was a muggy, still day in late August when Ben and Lucy decided to go for a trek up past the bluff and take Milliken with them. The city was hot and depressing. Lucy had never seen Papa so sad. He'd had some work to do in the country helping farmers with building projects, but not enough to support their family. The drought had ruined the gardens and fields of most farms in the area.

Although Richard continued hunting, he often came home empty-handed. The drought had driven the small game deeper into the dense forests and up into the hills, where spring water sustained them.

When Lucy and Ben took Milliken up into the woods, Lucy could forget the awful problems. On this day as they started out, little Timmy put up a terrible squall to go along. Usually Susannah distracted him or talked him out of it. But for once, Susannah seemed unable to cope.

"Perhaps this one time," she said, looking at Lucy and Ben with tired, pleading eyes.

Lucy knew that short-legged Tim would slow them

down and keeping an eye on him would be a worry. Taking Milliken was problem enough. But how could they say no?

"All right," Ben said. Lucy was glad he was the first to answer. "Come along." He reached out his hand, and Tim ran to grab it.

Down through the dry creek bed they went, Milliken bleating with joy at every step. Since following the creek bed was easier than walking through dry, prickly underbrush, they followed it awhile, then made their way up the other side to higher ground.

Usually the woods were much cooler, but today the heat penetrated through the green canopy of tall trees.

Lucy sang songs as they walked along. Timmy loved the boatmen songs and asked for them over and over. Usually Lucy could sing them all and never get tired, but today the air was so heavy, it was as though she couldn't get her breath. After an hour or so, they came to a clearing, and she suggested they tether Milliken and sit down.

"Milliken sure is producing milk," Ben said. "How long do you think it will last?" He pulled out the canteen he'd filled with well water and handed it to Lucy.

"I'm not sure. I'll have to ask Betsy." She took a swallow of the warm water and let it trickle down her dry throat. Timmy was fascinated with the way Milliken cropped the grass. He sat close by the goat, watching her every move.

Ben took back the canteen and offered it to Tim. "Just a few swallows, Timmy," he said. "We need it to last till we get back."

Tim nodded and tipped the canteen carefully.

Lucy loosened the strings of her bonnet. "I believe this has been the longest summer of my life." Sprawled out on the grass, she was painfully aware of how short her dress was becoming. She'd grown a few inches during the summer just as Ben had. But there'd be no new dresses for school.

Timmy looked up from watching Milliken. "I hear something."

Lucy sat very still for a moment. "I do, too. It's rumbling."

"Could it be. . .?" Ben asked.

"Thunder?" Lucy queried, jumping to her feet.

They couldn't see the horizon through the dense trees. The sky above them was still sunny and hazy blue.

"Let's go look!" Lucy pulled up the tether stick and pulled on Milliken, who wasn't ready to leave this lush pasture.

Ben came from behind and gave the goat a shove just as another rumble sounded. "It is, Lucy. It is thunder. I bet it's going to rain. And when it rains, the river will be up. . ."

"Hurry," Lucy interrupted with panic growing in her voice. "We've got to get home."

"Why? It's just rain. I want to be in the rain."

"I should have known from the heavy, still air," Lucy said, pulling on the goat's rope as hard as she could and heading quickly back the way they came. "It gets still like that before a bad storm. Papa's warned me, but I forgot. It hasn't rained for so long."

"I'm getting scared," Timmy said.

"Maybe we could find a cave," Ben suggested, taking hold of Timmy's hand and hurrying his step. "Richard says there're lots of caves out here."

"If we happen upon a cave, we'll sure crawl inside, but it's foolish to try to hunt for one."

Just then the crashing sound of thunder echoed above their heads and a cool wind swished through the tops of the trees. Milliken bolted, and Lucy nearly tumbled as she tried to follow.

"It's almost on us," Lucy called out.

Timmy began to cry, so Ben stopped to take him up piggyback. This slowed him some, while Milliken dragged Lucy on ahead. They were about halfway back to Deer Creek when they could see greenish-gray clouds boiling up in the west. Lucy felt two fat raindrops hit her face. So long they'd prayed for rain, and now it had arrived in a furious storm. It just didn't seem fair.

"See that big tree?" Ben called out. Rain was falling in gray sheets. "Let's get under there and stay."

"Let's do," Lucy answered. She pulled and tugged on the rope as Milliken kicked up her heels and bleated out her misery and fright. The sunlight was gone, and even though it was early afternoon, it was dim as dusk.

"I want my mama," Timmy cried as Ben set him down beneath the tree.

Lucy wished Timmy were back with his mama, but she didn't say so. After all, her own mama would be worried as well. Thunder crashed about them like giant cymbals from the marching band. It felt good to have the hard, pelting rain out of their faces. Lucy's petticoats clung to her ankles. She put her arms about Milliken's neck and tried to calm the frightened goat.

"I just remembered, Ben," Lucy said. "Papa said never to stay under a tree in a thunderstorm."

"Richard said something like that to me, too," Ben agreed. "But it's so bad right now we have no choice. We need to watch out for Timmy."

"Take me home," Timmy whined as he rubbed his eyes with his fists.

Just then a clap of thunder caused Milliken to leap in the air, and the wet rope slipped from Lucy's grasp.

"Oh no!" she cried. "Milliken, come back! Ben, help!"

Quickly Ben heaved Timmy up on his back. "Follow her, Lucy! We're right behind you."

Sliding on the wet leaves, Lucy sped out in the direction Milliken had taken. Thankfully, it was toward home.

The three had not gone more than a few yards when a blinding flash of light filled the air around them and a crash sounded so loud it made Lucy's ears ache. She turned to look and was aghast to see that the fierce lightning had sent the massive tree they had just been sitting under crashing to the ground.

Ben stopped as well. They were numb with shock.

"Ben," Lucy said, "I think Milliken just saved our lives."

"She did that all right." He adjusted the weight of the whimpering Timmy. "Hush now, Tim. It's all right. We're headed home." Then he laughed out loud. "Home," he repeated, "where Milliken will probably be waiting for us as if nothing had happened."

Lucy joined in the laughter, but her voice was all quivery. She couldn't wait to hug Milliken's neck. The rain had lessened some and the wind had calmed. By the time they reached Deer Creek, water was rushing freely down the creek bed. No more walking in the dry bed. They made their way to the rickety old bridge and crossed there.

The sight of flowing water thrilled Lucy. Maybe this meant there'd be river traffic soon.

Milliken was indeed waiting in the dooryard of the Allertons'. Susannah's look of relief when she met three drenched children at the door told how worried she'd been. She stoked up the cookstove and made them stand by it until they stopped shivering. Cups of hot cider helped take the chill off.

"Earlier today, I never thought I'd be cool again," Lucy said between chattering teeth. "Now look at me."

Susannah offered to let Lucy put on one of her old dresses, but Lucy insisted that she go on home so Mama wouldn't worry. But first they told Susannah the story of how Milliken saved their lives. Even Timmy helped add a few vivid details.

"Boom!" he said, flinging his hands in the air. "The big old tree went boom and fell down."

"If you hadn't chased out after the goat. . ." Susannah shook her head and bit her lower lip. "God watches after His own," she said. Her voice trembled as she spoke.

The welcome rains fell off and on for a number of days, until finally one morning Lucy heard the most beautiful sound. The melodious tones of a keeler blowing his tin horn echoed through the valley. She was eating breakfast when she first heard it.

She gobbled down her food and told Mama she was going to Ben's to help with Milliken. By the time she reached Ben's house, Milliken had been fed and was tethered at the edge of the clearing.

"Ben," Lucy said, "did you hear the horn?"

He nodded. "I did. At least the barges and keelboats can get through."

"Let's go see."

"See what?"

"The boats come in, silly."

"From the bluff?"

Lucy shook her head. "From the landing."

"But your mama won't like that much. We can watch from the bluff."

"From the bluff we can see them come downriver, but

91

only on the landing can we see them unload." She started out as though she expected him to follow. "It's been forever since a boat unloaded, and I don't want to miss it."

She could tell he was thinking about it, but in a moment he was by her side. "I hope we don't get into trouble," he said.

"Just for a little while. Then we'll come back and help Susannah with her chores."

Sure enough, three keelboats were at the landing. One was larger than the rest, with space for eight rowers for traveling upstream. This keelboat had a large, boxy cabin in the center where passengers could get shelter from the weather.

Lucy led Ben to an opening between a warehouse and the saddlery where they could see but not be seen. She made sure they stayed on the other side of the landing from the boatworks just in case Papa and George might be around. However, since work had come to a complete standstill, the men seldom came to the landing anymore.

From the talk on the landing, Lucy and Ben learned that these boats had come up from St. Louis just as soon as the rains began.

Suddenly Lucy gave a gasp. Emerging from the cabin of the larger boat was a lovely lady dressed in a fine traveling frock the color of moss in the woods. Her bonnet was lined with ruffles, and the bow was tied smartly beneath her proud chin. Long gloves graced her slender arms up to her elbows. She looked as though she'd stepped out of a fashion catalog from Lidell's store rather than from the cabin of a boat. Lucy could only stare with her mouth gaping.

CHAPTER 12
Sadie Rose

"Ben, do you see that lady?" Lucy asked in a whisper.

She looked over at Ben, who was bug-eyed as well. "I'm not blind," he said. "What do you suppose she's doing coming here? There's nothing in Cincinnati."

They waited a minute to see if a gentleman came to her side. A small crowd was gathering on the landing. The news had traveled that a trickle of river traffic had begun. Perhaps someone would come down to meet the well-dressed lady.

"Do you suppose she's traveling alone?" Lucy whispered.

Ben shook his head. "Impossible."

But the lady, with her head erect, proceeded to lift the skirt of her empire dress and walk across the running board of the boat to the gangplank.

"Maybe it's not so impossible," Lucy said. "She may have a good deal of money and she may need help with her bags." Pulling on Ben's sleeve, she said, "Follow me. Hurry."

"Lucy, we can't. . ."

"Then I'm going alone, and I'll have all the coins to myself."

Pushing through the crowd, she sensed Ben was on her heels. Boldly Lucy walked right up to the lady. Up close she was even more lovely, with cheeks as smooth and rosy as a fresh peach. Lucy could see she wore "paint" on her lips, making them more red than they really were. She'd heard stories about painted ladies. A little shiver ran up her spine.

"Hello, ma'am," Lucy said, suddenly wishing her dress were not so small and faded. "Welcome to Cincinnati. My name's Lucy Lankford. My father builds boats over at the boatworks down there." She waved toward the far end of the landing. Lucy didn't want this fine lady to think she was some waif from Sausage Row.

A smile made the picture-perfect face come alive beneath the delicate bonnet. "Well, good morning to you, Lucy. And who might this be?" She motioned to Ben, who stood at Lucy's elbow.

"Oh, this is Benjamin Allerton, my cousin. Well, sort of a distant cousin. But he's my friend, and you can call him Ben."

The lady adjusted her ruffled parasol and held out a dainty gloved hand. "Ben, Lucy. My name is Sadie Rose. I'm honored to make your acquaintance."

"Sadie Rose," Lucy said softly. "That's a beautiful name. Sadie Rose what?"

"Just Sadie Rose. It's enough, don't you think?"

"Oh yes, ma'am. It's perfect," Lucy replied. Why the lady even smelled like roses. "Where are you headed?" Lucy

94

asked, suddenly remembering her mission.

"I'm going to stay at Menessier's boarding house."

"Ben and I know right where that is. We can show you the way and carry your bags as well."

Again came the smile that seemed to light up the entire landing. "That's a kind offer," said Sadie Rose. She gave her reticule a little shake. Lucy could hear coins jingling. "Of course I'd make it worth your while. Wait here while I see about having my trunk carried up later."

Since the streets were still fairly muddy, Lucy deemed it best that they take Sadie Rose up Lawrence Street, which was not quite as steep as the others.

The bags were heavy, and before they were halfway to the boarding house, Lucy and Ben were puffing.

"I hope it's not too much for you," Sadie Rose said.

"Oh no, ma'am, not at all. Ben and I like to work. We work all the time. That is, we would work all the time if there were more work to do."

"I've heard your city has suffered hard times this summer."

"You heard the truth," Ben put in.

"How long are you staying?" Lucy asked between breaths.

Sadie Rose paused. "I'm undecided just now," she said.

Lucy knew it was rude to ask so many questions, but she couldn't help herself. She wanted to know everything about this lady. "How did you travel all that way by yourself with those ornery boatmen?" she asked.

"I paid for protection."

Lucy gave a little chuckle. "That's a smart plan."

Ben wasn't so sure. "I've heard of boatmen who've killed their passengers just to get the money," he said.

Sadie Rose stopped and looked at Ben. "Those passengers were probably snooty dandies from back East who thought they were better than those of us out West. You have to understand the boatmen in order to get along with them."

Lucy saw Ben's ears turn pink. He used to think anyone on this side of the Allegheny Mountains was some kind of mindless ruffian. But he was learning differently.

"Mrs. Menessier's boarding house sits at the end of this block, Miss Sadie Rose."

"Good. And you can just call me Sadie Rose. Plain and simple."

"Yes, ma'am, Sadie Rose," Lucy answered.

At the front porch of the boarding house, Ben and Lucy struggled to get the heavy bags up the steps. Once they did, Sadie Rose pulled open the reticule and placed two coins in each upturned palm. Lucy hadn't seen a coin for many months. It felt cool and solid in her fist. She looked at Ben and smiled. Now she could pay for the damaged hymnals at the church.

"May we show you anything else in town, Sadie Rose?" Lucy wanted to know. "After you've unpacked and settled in?"

"Why yes. Do you know a man by the name of Moses Brooks?"

Lucy felt Ben looking at her. "Yes, ma'am, I surely do. And I can take you right to the door of his place." Ben nudged her in the side with his elbow. She ignored him. "We'll be right here on the steps waiting for you, Sadie Rose."

"Thank you, children," replied the melodious voice. "How kind you are to a stranger."

Just then, the portly Mrs. Menessier appeared at the door, wiping her hands on her apron. "Ain't takin' no boarders, lessen you got real money," she said curtly. "No credit."

"Good morning, Mrs. Menessier," Lucy said, stepping forward.

"Well morning, Little Lucy. What are you doing around here?"

Ignoring the question, Lucy introduced Sadie Rose and assured the matron that Sadie Rose was good for the rent money.

Mrs. Menessier squinted at the immaculately dressed lady standing on her porch. "Very well, I'll take your word for it, Lucy." She pushed the door open farther and stepped back to let Sadie Rose inside.

When the women were out of earshot, Ben said, "Lucy Lankford, have you gone daft? We can't take her to a tavern! Especially a tavern on Front Street. Your Mama will tan your hide and hang it up to dry if she ever finds out."

"If she ever finds out. But she won't. And this money can pay for new hymnals at the church. And maybe even a little food, if there's any food left in the city to buy." Lucy sat down on the top step of the porch to wait. "These are desperate times, Benjamin. Desperate times call for desperate measures."

Once she'd said the words, she was pleased at how grown up it sounded. Maybe when she handed the money to Mama, she could say, "Now please don't call me 'Little Lucy' again." But how was she going to explain the money without telling a story? She'd have to think of something.

Ben, she could tell, was still stewing about going to a tavern on Front Street, but Lucy pretended not to notice. Presently, Sadie Rose came back out the door. Gone was the moss green traveling dress with matching jacket. Now there was a beautiful afternoon dress of the finest raspberry-colored taffeta Lucy had ever seen.

Jumping to her feet, Lucy said, "Sadie Rose, you're so beautiful."

Sadie Rose just smiled. "Thank you, Lucy. Now, shall we be on our way?"

"I've never heard of a lady traveling alone on a keelboat, and I never heard of a lady going alone to a tavern," Lucy said. "What will you do there?"

Sadie's lilting laughter bubbled like a little stream up in the hills. "By my leave, Lucy, you're about the most curious girl I've ever met. If you must know, I'm the new singer and piano player for Mr. Brooks."

Lucy felt her heart pick up a beat. She glanced over at Ben, whose eyebrows were raised. "You know how to play the piano?" Lucy asked.

"Been playing since I was knee high to a mosquito."

"And you sing?"

"Like a bird."

"Lucy sings," Ben said, hardly able to keep out of this conversation.

"Does she now?"

"Oh, Ben," Lucy said, but inwardly she was glad he'd told Sadie Rose.

"Yes, ma'am," Ben went on. "Last May she was chosen to sing at school commencement."

Last May seemed like such a long time ago to Lucy. The long hot summer had not been fun at all.

"If you're such a good singer," said Sadie, twirling her parasol, "let's hear you sing something."

Lucy never had to be asked twice. She burst out in a lively boatmen song. On the chorus, Sadie joined in, but moved a couple notes higher to harmonize perfectly.

When the song was over, Sadie Rose said, "Your cousin was right, Lucy. You do sing well."

"Thank you, Sadie Rose. Your voice is like an angel."

"An angel I am not, but I thank you kindly for the sentiments."

"Right down there is Brooks Tavern," Lucy said, pointing down Front Street.

"I see the sign," said Sadie. "You two can run on now." Again Lucy heard the lovely clink of coins. This time Sadie Rose handed each cousin a single coin. Now Lucy had three. She could hardly believe it.

"But you can't stay in this area alone," Ben insisted. "Don't you want us to walk you back?"

Sadie Rose touched Ben's shoulder lightly with her gloved hand. "Young Benjamin, what a gentleman you are. Thank you, but I need your help no longer today. Mr. Brooks will see to my safe journey back to the boarding house."

Lucy knew Sadie Rose would be singing at the tavern until the wee hours of the morning. Even in the worst of times, there still seemed to be business at the taverns, especially those down on Front Street. Papa said when times get hard, men either prayed or drank. Lucy was thankful her papa prayed.

As she and Ben trudged back through the muddy streets toward home, Lucy could hardly keep still. She wanted to laugh and sing and shout. What a splendid day it had turned out to be!

"I can hardly believe such a fine lady would sing at a tavern," Ben was saying.

"There's nothing wrong with singing at a tavern," Lucy said in defense of her new friend. But she wasn't sure she was right. She'd heard stories about men fighting and killing one another after becoming drunk at a tavern. One thing she knew for sure—Sadie Rose was a very nice lady.

As she and Ben passed through the edge of Sausage Row,

the smells were awful. Sewage and garbage lined the streets. Houses were little more than shacks, nothing like the fine brick home Lucy's papa had built for his family. Vacant buildings with boarded-up windows bore testimony of the hard times in the city.

"I suppose we should have gone up to Second Street," Ben said, wrinkling his nose.

Lucy silently agreed. Although there might be garbage in other parts of the city, nothing ever smelled as bad as Sausage Row. In her apron pocket were her three coins. She held them tightly in her fist and kept her hand in the pocket.

"What are you going to tell your mama about the money?" Ben asked.

He must have been reading her thoughts. She was wondering the same thing. "Why, I'll just tell her the truth. That a boat came in, we went to watch, and then we carried bags for a passenger."

Ben nodded. "I guess that sounds fine, but she doesn't like you going to the landing."

"Perhaps the sight of the money will make it all right. What will you tell Richard and Susannah?"

"Richard has never forbidden me to go to the landing. . ."

Just then, a terrible ruckus in an alleyway behind the vacant buildings broke into their conversation.

"Give that back!" they heard a voice yell. "That's mine. Give it back!"

"Someone's in trouble," Lucy said.

"Stay out of it, Lucy." Ben tugged at her arm, but she pulled away.

"That voice sounds like Raggy." She stopped to listen. "It sounds like he's dying. We've got to do something, Ben. Follow me."

100

CHAPTER 13

A Visit with Charlotte

Lucy backtracked and made her way carefully around a vacant warehouse, hoping Ben was right behind her. Peeking around the corner, she saw two boys, bigger than Raggy, who were taunting him. She motioned for Ben to come beside her and look.

"You stay here," she said softly. "I'm going around the other way. When I give the signal, dive for their knees."

When she arrived at the opposite corner of the building, she could see the boys had something that Raggy desperately wanted. Strangely enough, it appeared to be a piece of blue flowered cloth.

"Rag-gee, Rag-gee," the boys taunted. "Carries his rag with him wherever he goes." The taller boy waved the cloth in front of Raggy like a flag. Just as Raggy leaped to grab it, the boy passed it off to his friend. There were tears in Raggy's eyes.

When Lucy saw Ben peek his head around the corner, she waved her hand. The two of them ran, each one toward one of the tormenters, and slammed them as hard as they could in the back of the knees with their shoulders. Both boys tumbled to the ground. In a flash, Raggy grabbed the cloth and fled, disappearing around the corner of the building.

"Why you yellow-bellied little twerps," one boy growled as he struggled to his feet. "I'll grind you to bits and feed you to the crows."

"Come on, Ben," Lucy said. "Let's get out of here." But she was quickly and roughly grabbed from behind.

"Not so quick, little girl," the second boy said. "You're gonna pay for buttin' in where you ain't welcome."

"Pay?" Lucy said. Reaching into her pocket, she pulled out two of her precious coins. "Look here," she said. "I'll pay."

"Money!" the first boy exclaimed. "She has real money."

"And it's all yours!" Lucy yelled as she flung the coins as far as she could.

Immediately she was released, while the boys scrambled to retrieve the money. She and Ben made their getaway, leaving Sausage Row far behind.

When they were in their own safe neighborhood once again, they slowed their pace. Still heaving to catch his breath, Ben handed Lucy two of his three coins and said, "Here, Lucy. I want you to have these."

She pushed his hand away and shook her head. "You earned that money fair and square. In fact, I want you to take my last one and keep it, too. There's not enough to pay for hymnals anyway."

Ben solemnly took the coin. "I'll keep it for you, but it's still yours."

Lucy nodded.

They walked along in silence for a time. Then Ben ventured to say, "I thought you didn't like Raggy Wallace, but you helped him. That doesn't make much sense to me."

"I guess I just don't like to see bullies win, no matter who the bullies are."

That night at supper, Papa seemed in better spirits than he'd been for many weeks. "With a few keelboats getting through, perhaps trade will begin to pick up," he said. "We'll pray the fall rains come early and are plentiful. Before you know it, the landing could be booming once again."

Mama had cooked up a kettle of the dried beans Papa had brought back from one of the farmers for whom he'd worked. At least it was a change from the steady diet of salt pork and cornbread. Lucy noticed that Papa was always careful to say a blessing over their meals, no matter how little they had.

As they were eating, Mama shared her good news as well. A letter had arrived from Betsy saying she and Andrew would be coming for a visit and would bring as many provisions as they could. "Eggs and cheese," Mama said, closing her eyes. "How good that will taste. Maybe a watermelon. Mm."

Later that night Lucy lay tossing about in her bed. The hot August night made sleeping difficult. Not a bit of breeze fluttered through her dormer windows. Lucy couldn't seem to get the look of Raggy's sad face from her mind. It was a puzzle. Why would Raggy Wallace fight two bigger boys for a little piece of flowered cloth? Although she still didn't trust Raggy, suddenly he didn't seem like such a threat anymore.

A couple times during the summer, Lucy had received permission from Mama to walk to Charlotte's house, or rather to the cabin where the Hendricks now lived. Since it was situated far on the west side of town, Mama didn't like Lucy to go there alone. But when Ben could go along, Mama was more willing.

Even though Lucy loved Charlotte, it made her sad to visit the small cabin and to see that the family didn't have many of the nice things they used to have. Mr. Hendricks had owned a lot of land, and when prices plummeted, suddenly he lost not only his money in the bank, but his land as well.

On this day, Lucy and Ben were taking a bag of dried beans to the family. The streets were once again thick layers of powdery dust, and the sun bore down hotter than ever. Perhaps Papa's prediction for early fall rain was overly hopeful.

On the way across town, Lucy insisted they go by the boarding house in hopes of seeing Sadie Rose. Lucy desperately wanted to see her new friend once again. She bravely knocked on the front door and asked to see Sadie Rose, but Mrs. Menessier glared at her sternly.

"There'd be no reason for a girl like you to visit with the likes of Sadie Rose, Little Lucy. You can't see her anyway because she's asleep. She sleeps most of the day. Every day. Even Sundays!" With that she closed the door.

Lucy was indignant. "The likes of Sadie Rose," she muttered as they walked away. "What a terrible way to talk."

"She didn't mean anything by it," Ben replied. "Remember, Lucy, most people don't approve of ladies who spend time in a tavern."

"But Sadie Rose is different."

"From what?"

Lucy shrugged. After all, what did she know about ladies

in taverns? "I don't know. She's just different, that's all."

Thankfully Ben didn't argue. He never did.

The Hendricks's cabin sat in a clearing near Mill Creek. Charlotte was sitting under a shade tree in the front yard, watching her new baby sister and sewing a patch on a pair of John's trousers. Her little sister Mercy played in the dirt nearby.

A smile lit her face when she saw the pair approaching. Jumping up, she ran to give Lucy a hug. "How good to see you again. I miss you awfully." After grabbing up the baby and taking Mercy's hand, she led them inside.

Mrs. Hendricks greeted Ben and Lucy graciously and offered to fix them each a cup of dandelion tea. Though Lucy didn't care for dandelion tea, she didn't want to be rude, so she said yes.

Lucy wished she and Charlotte could visit alone like old times at school. If only their families attended the same church, at least she'd see her friend on Sundays. Lucy wanted to tell her about Sadie Rose and describe her fashionable frocks and bonnets. She wanted to tell her about seeing Raggy crying over a little piece of flowered cloth.

But a private conversation was impossible. As usual, the visit would be short. Mrs. Hendricks was grateful for the beans, but Lucy could tell it was an embarrassment to the woman to accept them and to Charlotte as well. They had had so much, and now they had virtually nothing. The very thought made Lucy's heart ache.

Later that afternoon back at Ben's house, he showed Lucy the stanchion he'd constructed. "See how it works?" He demonstrated by moving back and forth the slat that would hold Milliken's head firm as she was milked. They'd been tying Milliken's head close to a post when they milked her, but the goat moved around more than they'd like.

"Let's try it out," Lucy suggested.

Together they went to the edge of the clearing. Ben lifted the tether out of the ground, and they led the goat to the stanchion. It was a perfect fit.

"Get a bucket," Lucy instructed.

Ben did so and brought her the T-shaped stool he'd made. Lucy situated herself beside the goat, just as she'd done for weeks. She firmly grasped the teats and began to pull. "Ben! It works like a charm."

Streams of milk flowed into the bucket as Milliken stood still. For once, they weren't losing quarts of milk because of Milliken's hooves bumping the bucket. Even quiet Ben grew excited.

"Susannah," he called out. "Come and see. The stanchion works!"

After Susannah and the children had watched Lucy and Ben take turns milking Milliken, Lucy turned to Susannah and asked, "Milliken is giving so much milk, do you think we could make some goat's cheese?"

"What a fine idea," Susannah said. "I know just where my cheesecloths and wheels are packed away."

"Susannah," Lucy called as the young woman turned toward the house.

"Yes," Susannah said.

"Could we keep this a secret from my parents? I'd like to surprise them."

Susannah smiled. "Of course, Lucy. Now let's get to work."

Several days later, the cheese-making process was complete.

Lucy insisted that Susannah keep part of it for her own family. Susannah wrapped the remainder of the cheese in some cloth and placed it in a stone jar for Lucy to carry home.

Later, when Mama and Papa tasted the soft cheese spread on some cornbread, Lucy studied their faces.

"Mm-mm," Papa said as he set his cup down. "That's about the best cheese I've ever tasted in my life. What do you think, Ellie?"

Lucy was surprised to see tears brimming in Mama's eyes. "I do believe Little Lucy is growing up, Paul. It's a big job to care for a goat, then milk her and make cheese as well."

What beautiful words to Lucy's ears. She ran to Mama's side and gave her a hearty hug.

A few days later, the Farley's buckboard came rumbling up the street in front of the Lankford home, and Lucy ran out the front door to greet them.

Their wagon was laden with bags and barrels. A wicker basket held a fat watermelon, along with a few cucumbers, carrots, and turnips. In a crate were two cackling chickens. Thoughts of tasty chicken and dumplings made Lucy's mouth water. Finally, something to eat other than salt pork!

CHAPTER 14

A Summer Feast

"Milliken's giving lots of milk," Lucy cried out as she ran around to Betsy's side of the wagon. "We've even made cheese."

Andrew secured the brake on the wagon. Laughing, he said, "Well, well. Hello to you, Lucy. Good to see you."

"Lucy Lankford," Mama corrected, "what an improper greeting." To Andrew and Betsy she said, "I dare say this child has totally lost all decorum this summer. Everything has been at loose ends."

"Please, Ellie," Betsy said, "don't apologize. We love Lucy's exuberance." She patted her large tummy. "I hope my little one is made of the same cloth."

Andrew jumped down and came around to assist his

wife. While Papa helped Andrew unload the wagon, the women went inside to catch up on all the latest news.

George and Patricia, as well as Richard, Susannah, and the children, were invited for Sunday dinner. It would be a celebration. A summer feast! Lucy was ecstatic.

Later that evening, Betsy went along with Lucy to Ben's house. When they arrived, Ben had just brought the goat in from her tether. Susannah and the children came out to greet Betsy, and together they all went out back so Betsy could see Milliken.

Betsy could hardly believe how well the goat looked. "I don't believe Millie is this big," she said, petting Milliken's head and rubbing her ears. "You've taken such good care of her, Lucy. I'm so proud of you."

"Mama didn't think I could do it," Lucy said, stretching to stand a little taller.

Betsy nodded. "Sometimes mamas are the last ones to realize their babies are growing up." She smiled. "I'll probably be the same way."

"But I didn't do it all by myself." Lucy reached out and grabbed Ben's arm, pulling him forward from where he'd been standing behind them. "Ben helped a lot."

"I'm guessing he built the enclosure and the stanchion."

"You guessed right," Lucy said.

Betsy ran her hands over the wooden stanchion. "What splendid workmanship," she said.

Susannah agreed. "Ben's a good worker, and he's a gifted carpenter."

Then they all laughed as Ben blushed and ducked his head.

On Saturday, Andrew wanted to see the steamboats, so the

men left to go to the boatworks. The women butchered chickens and set them to boiling. Pies were baked and turnips stewed. The kitchen was unbearably hot, but no one seemed to mind.

Seeing and smelling all the scrumptious food made Lucy think about Charlotte in her crowded cabin. How she wished Charlotte and her family could share in this feast. The more she thought about it, the better she liked the idea. But since this was a family gathering, she wasn't at all sure Mama would agree.

Mama, however, did agree. "Why, Little Lucy, what a kind heart you have," she said. Mama dumped a basket of dried apples into an iron kettle of boiling water. Later those sweet apples would be the filling for a juicy apple pie. Setting the basket down, Mama said, "We have more than enough food for the Hendricks to join us. You and Ben run over to Charlotte's and extend the invitation."

"Ben's gone off with Richard today, Mama. But I can go by myself."

Mama hesitated. She reached up to take her large stirring spoon down from its hook and stirred the apples thoughtfully.

"If I don't go, how will they ever know they're invited?" Lucy reasoned.

"I suppose you're right."

Lucy's heart skipped a beat. At last Mama was beginning to trust her. "I'll fetch my bonnet," she said.

"Tell them we'll expect them at three," Mama said.

"I'll tell them." Grabbing her bonnet and tying it beneath her chin, she said, "I'll be back before supper."

"See that you are," Mama answered. "Don't dillydally."

The look on Mrs. Hendricks's face when Lucy offered the

invitation was a sight to behold. Charlotte, too, fairly fluttered with excitement.

"There's plenty, and we want you to come and be with us," Lucy assured them.

"I don't know how to thank you." Mrs. Hendricks stood at her doorway with the baby resting on her hip. She'd invited Lucy inside, but Lucy declined the offer. She had to hurry back home.

"Your family has been more than kind to us," Mrs. Hendricks went on. "John and Mr. Hendricks are grateful as well. We'll come along to your home directly from church."

"We'll be expecting you around three." With a wave, Lucy turned back down the path. At last she and Charlotte would have a few minutes alone to talk.

The air was steamy hot, and Lucy was grateful for the shade from her bonnet. How she wished she had a fancy dress with a matching parasol to ward off the hot sun.

When she arrived back in town, she made sure her path led past the boarding house. There on the front porch sat Sadie Rose! Lucy could hardly believe her good fortune. Sadie Rose was dressed in a pink ruffled frock with billowy sleeves and no bonnet. In her hand she held an ivory fan, which she waved slowly back and forth.

Lucy nearly ran in Sadie's direction. "Hello," she called out. "Hello, Sadie Rose."

Sadie Rose's lovely face broke into a smile that warmed Lucy's heart. "Hello to you, Lucy. Come up and set a spell. How have you been?"

Lucy bounded up the steps to the porch and sat down in the wicker chair beside Sadie Rose. "I'm quite well, thank you. I stopped by to see you one day, but Mrs. Menessier said you were sleeping."

Sadie laughed lightly. "Ah yes, sleep. Something I do when others are awake."

"Are you still singing at Mr. Brooks's tavern?"

"That I am. Mr. Brooks, it turns out, is as fair an employer as I've had in quite a spell."

"I'm pleased to hear that."

"He appreciates my singing and my piano music."

"I'm sure you're excellent." Lucy had so many questions to ask. "Sadie, how did you learn to play the piano? Did you take lessons?"

Sadie Rose adjusted her ruffled skirts and gave a little sigh. "It was my dear ma who taught me. Before she died."

"Oh, I'm sorry," Lucy said.

"No need to be sorry. It was such a long time ago."

"Sadie, would it be too much to ask. . .I mean, well, I was supposed to have a piano. It was ordered, but the bank failures and the dried-up river slowed everything down."

Sadie Rose closed her fan and leaned forward. "Yes, Lucy? What is it you want to ask?"

"Could you teach me a little bit about the piano? Just a little? I wouldn't take up much of your time."

Sadie relaxed back into her chair. "Why, of course I could teach you. At least a couple songs anyway. Meet me at the tavern early next Saturday morning. No one will be there then. Can you make it?"

"But I thought you slept late."

"Lucy, for you I'd sacrifice my sleep."

For a moment Lucy thought her heart would beat right out of her chest. "Thank you, Sadie Rose. I'll be there next Saturday morning."

Lucy ran the rest of the way home and barely made it before the family sat down to supper.

Sunday's feast was a magnificent affair. Because Mama's table wasn't nearly big enough, makeshift tables were set up in the dining room by placing long boards over sawhorses. John and Ben took their plates out in the dooryard to eat. Timmy, Pamela, and Charlotte's sister, Mercy, were fed in the kitchen. But Lucy and Charlotte were allowed to eat with the grown-ups.

The men talked of better times and how wise banking practices could prevent such disasters from ever hitting Cincinnati again. At one point during the meal, Lucy was surprised to hear Richard say to Papa, "Paul, I want you to know I've changed my mind about working at the boatworks with you and George."

Papa's bushy eyebrows went up, but he waited for Richard to have his say.

"I've been doing a good deal of thinking this summer," Richard went on. "It always seemed to me a man could make a go of things by himself. Well, I've tried that, and I've seen my family go without the things they need."

"We've all seen our families go without," came Papa's gentle reply.

"That's true," Richard said. "The difference is, you have something to go back to. I don't. I know the economy will turn around and the river won't be dry forever. I'd have to be blind not to see that steamboats are the coming thing." He paused a moment, and Lucy knew that Richard was struggling to say what his heart felt. "If the offer's still good, I'm ready to take you up on it."

It was George who answered. "The offer's as good as the day it was given."

Richard nodded. "Thank you, George. As soon as you can take me on, let me know, and I'll be there."

After dinner, Papa took down his fiddle, and Lucy stood up a few steps on the stairway in the hall and sang for everyone. Soon she had them all clapping their hands and laughing and joining in on the choruses. Hearts that had been heavy with worry and fear were made lighter for having a few hours of fun.

Because Lucy and Charlotte were put in charge of all the little ones while the women cleared the tables and washed dishes, there still was no time for quiet talk. But Lucy realized she wasn't quite ready to tell Charlotte about Sadie Rose. Instead they talked about the opening of school, which was set for the next week.

Charlotte said she didn't care that she didn't have pretty dresses for the new school term. "I'm just anxious to get back to studying," she said. "Mama and Papa and John and I have all agreed that things aren't nearly as important as having one another."

Lucy thought about that a moment and realized she agreed. Even though she still longed to have her own piano, she knew a piano could never replace the love of her family.

Andrew and Betsy left before dawn the next morning. As the empty wagon rattled noisily down the street, Lucy waved and hollered her good-byes, remembering especially to say thank you over and over again. She wondered what her family would have done without the generosity of the Farleys.

With the new stock of foodstuffs in the larder, Papa was sure they could make it through until things turned around, which he believed would be very soon.

Mama and Susannah continued to make cheese with the extra milk, and of course there was plenty for everyone to drink. Even George and Patricia took a share.

114

All week, Lucy stewed about in her mind, trying to think of a way she could meet Sadie Rose at the tavern on Saturday morning. In the end, the problem took care of itself. It was Mama who suggested that Lucy take a jar of goat's milk to the dressmaker to see if she could trade for a ribbon and lace.

Mama had been rummaging in the chest of clothing in the attic. Out of it she'd pulled two of her own cast-off dresses. "I believe," she said to Lucy, "there's enough cloth here to make you a proper school dress. All we need is new ribbon and lace." She gave Lucy small snippets of the fabric to match the colors.

Lucy could hardly believe her good fortune. If it were not for balancing the full jar of milk, she would have skipped all the way to the dressmaker's shop.

Mrs. Betts was pleased to be paid with fresh milk. Soon Lucy had the silky ribbon and delicate lace tucked away in her pocket, and bidding Mrs. Betts good day, she made her way down the hill to Brooks Tavern. As she did, she kept glancing around, hoping no one watching knew her or Papa.

Before she approached the tavern, she heard the enchanting sound of lilting piano music and the clear, full tones of Sadie Rose's singing. She stopped outside to listen, not wanting to break the spell. It was a hauntingly sad ballad about love being lost. Lucy stood entranced, wanting the song to go on forever. When the last note died away, she tapped on the door.

"Is that you, Lucy?"

"Yes, ma'am. It's me."

"The door's open. Come in."

Pushing open the door, Lucy wrinkled her nose at the heavy odor of beer that hung in the air. She'd often caught the aromas outside a tavern, but inside they were a hundred times worse. She hoped it wouldn't make her sick. Across the darkened room, she could see Sadie sitting at the piano.

A little shiver ran up Lucy's spine as she entered the forbidden tavern. She knew if Mama and Papa ever found out, they would never understand.

CHAPTER 15
Piano Lessons

"Come on over here and have a seat," Sadie Rose invited. "It's so good to see you again."

Sadie Rose pulled a chair next to the piano stool. Sitting so close to Sadie Rose, Lucy could catch whiffs of the fragrance of roses. Roses smelled much better than beer.

Pointing to a key in the center of the keyboard, Sadie told her it was called "middle C." Then she explained the octaves and taught her the eight notes in each octave.

"What about the black keys?" Lucy wanted to know.

"We call them sharps and flats," she said. "I'll tell you more about them in your next lesson."

Next lesson! What beautiful words to Lucy's ears.

"Do you recognize this melody?" Sadie asked. She placed

117

her right hand on the keys and picked out a simple tune.

"Why that's 'A Mighty Fortress Is Our God.' My favorite hymn."

"Is it now? It's my favorite, too. It's one of the first songs my ma ever taught me. Look how easy this is. It begins on this C up here and ends on middle C down here." Patiently, Sadie Rose pointed out the notes and then let Lucy follow her. Within minutes, Lucy had the first few bars down pat.

"I don't play this song very often anymore."

"Why not?" Lucy asked. "It's so beautiful."

"It brings back too many painful memories," Sadie Rose said wistfully.

"About your ma?"

Sadie Rose nodded. "When Ma and Pa died, my baby brother and I were given over to an orphanage in Philadelphia. It wasn't a very nice place, Lucy. I did my best to look out for little Thomas, but I had a difficult time of it."

"Ben's an orphan," Lucy offered. "He came here from Boston to live with his older brother. I'm sure glad he didn't have to live in an orphanage."

"Yes, be very thankful," Sadie replied, giving Lucy's shoulder a gentle pat. "Before Ma and Pa died, I gave them my word that I would always look after Thomas." Sadie paused and pulled a hankie from out of the sleeve of her blue organdy dress.

"What happened, Sadie Rose? What happened to Thomas?"

"People came," she said in the barest whisper. "Came and adopted him. They. . .they didn't want me. I said I could take care of him myself, but they laughed at me."

Lucy squeezed her eyes tight to blink back the hot tears. "That's so terrible," she said. "But you couldn't help what happened."

"But I promised. I promised Ma and Pa. Now I can't even get their forgiveness."

"No," Lucy agreed, "but you can surely get God's forgiveness if you just ask. And that's even better."

As though she hadn't heard, Sadie Rose went on. "The couple who took Thomas away said they were coming out West. I've traveled from town to town looking for him. That's why I sing in taverns." Sadie dabbed gently at the corners of her eyes. "It earns me enough money to keep on going."

"Why not pray and ask God to help? God knows where your brother is."

"Oh, Lucy, you're such a good, sweet girl. But I've forgotten how to pray. It's been so long."

The way Sadie Rose talked to Lucy made her feel much older than her ten, almost eleven, years. "Well, I haven't forgotten. Papa reads the Bible every evening, and we pray before going to bed. I can pray for you."

Sadie Rose's face lit up with a bright smile. "Oh, would you truly? I'd like that very much."

"Bow your head," Lucy directed. Then she very simply asked God to show Sadie Rose where and how to find her brother, Thomas. Then she added, "And please, Lord, let it happen quickly so Sadie Rose can stop wandering from place to place. In Jesus' name, amen."

Sadie Rose put her arm about Lucy's shoulder and gave her a squeeze. "Oh, Lucy, you're a good friend. I'm so glad you came to the landing the day I arrived. And I'm pleased to be able to help you learn to play the piano."

They continued working on the melody together until Lucy had it down pat. "Next time, I'll show you how to add chords with the left hand."

"I'd better go now. Mama's expecting me." Lucy made

119

her way to the back door and gave Sadie a little wave. "Bye now. And thank you very much."

"Thank you, Lucy."

With that Lucy slipped out and hurried up the hill. She hugged herself with happiness. She'd actually played a hymn on the piano. And almost as wonderful was the fact that the lovely Sadie Rose had confided in her. She promised herself that she would remember to pray for Sadie Rose every night.

If I were an orphan searching for my younger brother, she thought, perhaps I would sing in a tavern as well. Sadie's only doing what she has to do.

Lucy was scolded for arriving home late, but she didn't mind. Being with Sadie Rose was worth all the scoldings in the world.

September days were no cooler than August days had been. Sitting in the steamy, crowded classroom at school was sheer torture. Mr. Flinn's collar and tie were rumpled by mid-morning each day. Periodically he ran his finger around inside the stiff collar as though he wished he could fling it off.

So many things had changed since last spring. Charlotte was quieter, and she had no new dress to wear. Although Lucy's dress wasn't actually new, still it was prettier than almost any other dress in the classroom. How thankful she was she had a resourceful mama.

Benjamin now attended school upstairs. Lucy missed having him nearby, but she knew he'd be fine. He wasn't a dapper Boston dandy anymore. In fact, at first glance, he looked no different than any other boy at school. His face had lost its pasty color and fairly glowed from a summer of traipsing through the woods.

And, of course, John Hendricks was in the classroom

upstairs, too. He'd keep an eye out for Ben.

Raggy had also graduated to the upstairs classroom, but he attended seldom. Lucy had heard that Willie and Gus had both left town. Lucy thought Raggy looked thinner. If the depression had been hard on her family, she could only imagine what it was like for youngsters like Raggy.

As often as possible, Lucy stopped by the boarding house in hopes of seeing Sadie Rose. In the afternoons, she might be sitting on the porch catching a late afternoon breeze. Lucy would stop to talk with her. Little by little, she was coming to know her friend better. And it was a true friendship. Lucy had never had a grown-up for a friend before.

Ben never liked the idea of Lucy spending time at the tavern, yet he offered to stay with her each Saturday morning when she went for her lesson. Each time they took a different route so that, hopefully, no nosy person would see and report them to her papa.

"Mind you," Ben would say, "the more times you go to the tavern, the greater the chance of your being caught."

Lucy knew he was concerned for her, but she knew that Ben also liked to be around Sadie Rose. And who could blame him? How could anyone not like such a gracious and lovely lady?

September was drawing to a close when one cool Saturday morning she and Ben were sent to the market. While crops were much smaller than usual, still farmers were bringing in a smattering of fall produce corn, pumpkins, and squash. Some of the farmers would trade for goat's milk and cheese. Others wouldn't. After selecting three nice squash and several ears of corn, Lucy and Ben carried their basket down the hill and stopped at the tavern for a few moments.

By now Lucy could play all of "A Mighty Fortress" without making a single mistake. Sadie Rose seemed as thrilled as Lucy. "I believe you're a natural, Lucy. Soon we'll start on another song. Perhaps you'd like to learn a boatman song next."

"I'd like that, Sadie Rose," Lucy replied. "Lively boatmen songs make my feet want to dance a jig."

Sadie laughed. "I feel the same way."

"Lucy," Ben said to her. "We'd better get home." He was standing by the door with the basket sitting by his feet. "Your mama will have a conniption fit."

"He's right, you know," Sadie said. "You don't want to worry your ma."

Lucy was always reluctant to leave. When she was sitting at the piano with Sadie Rose, she forgot everything else.

Up the street they went with the basket between them. "Step lively," Ben said. "Your mama's expecting us."

Suddenly, from behind them came a loud whoop. Lucy dropped her hold on the basket and whirled around. There came Raggy, bearing down as fast and hard as he could run. He slammed into Benjamin, knocking him to the ground and making the basket fly. With one swipe, he grabbed two of the squash and kept on running.

"Come back here with that, you thief," Lucy yelled. "Come on, Ben. I bet we can catch him."

"Let him go." Ben gathered ears of corn and put them back into the basket.

"Let him go?"

"He's hungry, Lucy. Let him have the squash." He walked to the side of the street where the third squash had rolled. He brushed it off and placed it in the basket as well. "Come on. Let's go home."

"What'll we tell Mama?"

"That doesn't seem to be my concern," Ben said almost curtly.

"Are you upset with me?" she asked. She couldn't bear to have Ben angry with her.

"We shouldn't have been in this neighborhood with our purchases."

"But don't forget, Raggy Wallace stole from us one time when we were in our own neighborhood."

Ben was quiet for a moment. Then he said, "He never stole anything, Lucy. Remember? He grabbed the cloth, but he didn't keep it."

She knew Ben was right about Raggy and about the area of town they were walking in, but she didn't care. She wanted to be with Sadie Rose, and that was that. "If you don't want to come with me to the tavern anymore, then don't. I don't care."

"But your mama trusts me to be with you, so I don't have much choice, do I?"

Now that the basket was lighter, Lucy let Ben carry it alone. She walked on ahead, not wanting to talk.

At the Lankford front gate, they divided the ears of corn, then she made him take the last squash. Ben did as she asked and went on his way.

When Lucy stepped into the kitchen, Mama stood in front of her, an accusing look in her eyes.

Lucy wondered how Mama could possibly know about their mishap with Raggy so quickly.

But Mama wasn't concerned about the produce from the market. "Lucy Lankford," she said sternly. "I've had a visit from Widow Tuthill and two other ladies from the church. They came to tell me you've been seen spending time at the boarding house with a painted lady!" Mama's face looked tired. "Tell me, Lucy. Tell me it isn't true."

123

CHAPTER 16

Helping with the Rent

"It's true that I've been visiting with a lady by the name of Sadie Rose," Lucy said. "But she's not a bad person." Why couldn't old Widow Tuthill mind her own business? Lucy wondered as she put the ears of corn on the table.

"How on earth did you meet such a woman?" Mama wanted to know.

Lucy didn't want to lie. "The day the keelboats came up from St. Louis after the big rain, I asked Ben to go with me to the landing."

Mama sighed deeply and sat down on one of the kitchen chairs.

"The lady needed help, so we carried her bags. She was beholden to us, Mama. We showed her the way to Mrs. Menessier's boarding house. And you know Mrs. Menessier's

124

is a respectable place."

But Mama was shaking her head. "The landing can be a dangerous place for a little girl."

"I'm not a little girl, Mama. And Ben was with me."

"Then Ben should have reminded you of the dangers."

Lucy thought of all the times Ben had followed her into situations that were not of his choosing. He'd been a good friend, and she didn't want to get him into trouble as well.

"I take all the blame," Lucy said. "I shouldn't have been at the landing. But please believe me, Sadie Rose is not a bad lady."

"You keep telling me that you're not a little girl, and yet I find you've been disobedient and that you've been keeping undesirable company behind my back."

Mama smoothed back wisps of her hair, which Lucy noticed was growing much grayer. "When I must learn of my daughter's wrong behavior from others in the church. . ." Mama didn't finish the sentence. She stood up and walked over to the corn and began to pull off the shucks.

"I'll talk this over with your papa this evening. I know he will agree with me that you are forbidden to spend time with this woman. This, this Sadie Rose."

When Mama said the name, it sounded like something awful and made Lucy feel hurt and angry. But she kept her anger to herself. Somehow she had to make Mama understand about Sadie Rose.

Lucy talked to Sadie Rose one more time to tell her what had happened. Sadie Rose gave a kind smile. "I understand, Lucy. Your mama's looking out for you in the best way she knows how. You obey her and be thankful to have such a good mama."

Sadie Rose's words made Lucy want to cry. How could things be so mixed up?

In late November, the farmers brought their pigs into town to the packing houses. The air was filled with the frenzied sounds of hundreds of squealing pigs. At least the packing houses would be busy, which meant the tanners and chandlers and soap makers would soon have work. Papa said that little rebounds in business were better than no rebounds at all.

After the first snow, Ben bagged his first deer. Lucy went to see the carcass, which was hanging in a tree. It was a big buck, and Ben told her he was going to hang the antlers over his bed in the loft right beside the portraits of his mother and father. Lucy never remembered seeing Ben so proud or so happy.

Several of his delicately carved boats now lined the mantle over the Allerton fireplace. Lucy heard Susannah repeatedly praise Ben for his skills in woodworking. Ben didn't seem so sad anymore.

Just as Lucy's family had shared their provisions with Richard and Susannah, the Allertons now shared cuts of venison with the Lankfords. Thanksgiving dinner consisted mainly of game that had been killed by Richard and Ben.

Although it was difficult, Lucy remained obedient and didn't stop to visit with Sadie Rose. However, she often saw her friend about town. When she did, Lucy always stopped to say hello. Or she purposely walked by the boarding house in hopes of "accidentally" running into Sadie Rose. In her mind, one little greeting broke no rules. By keeping a close watch and by timing her walks by Mrs. Menessier's, Lucy continued to see Sadie Rose regularly.

While the citizens of Cincinnati knew that deep snow

meant a full river in the spring, still the hard winter only increased the suffering of those who were in need.

Lucy celebrated her eleventh birthday during a January snowstorm. Even though there was no party, Mama and Papa tried to make the day as special as they could. Lucy thought being eleven would be so much different, but everyone still called her Little Lucy.

It was mid-February when Lucy realized she'd not seen Sadie Rose for about two weeks. The heavy snows of January were melting some, and even though it was still cold, at least a person could walk down the streets without wading knee-deep in snow drifts.

Every day for a week, Lucy made Ben walk home from school by way of the boarding house. Still there was no sign of Sadie Rose. Finally Lucy could stand it no more.

"I must ask about her," Lucy insisted one afternoon after school. "There's no harm in asking, is there?"

"I don't see that there is," Ben answered.

Her cousin now stood nearly half a head taller than Lucy. Susannah often said she was going to load bricks on Ben's head to stop him from growing so fast. But he just kept growing. More and more, Lucy appreciated Ben's opinions and his quiet wisdom.

"Would you come with me?" she asked.

To her relief, he agreed. Lucy tightened her woolen muffler about her neck to better fight the cold wind as they went the few blocks out of their way to the boarding house.

Lucy went right up and rapped on the door, and Ben stood by her side.

When Mrs. Menessier opened the door, she said, "I suppose you're looking for Miss Sadie Rose."

"Why yes, we are," Lucy answered. "Is she here?"

The matron of the boarding house nodded. "She's here, but she's doing poorly. Been down with the fever and chills."

Lucy gave a gasp. "I knew something was wrong. May we see her?"

"I can't stop her from having visitors."

Lucy waited for Ben to protest, but he was quiet. Together they followed Mrs. Menessier inside and through a neat parlor area to the curved staircase. Waving to the stairs, she said, "Second door on the right."

As they started up the steps, Lucy heard Mrs. Menessier mutter something about "getting better soon" and "late with the rent." Lucy glanced back at Ben and could see he was as concerned as she.

Lucy tapped on the door and heard a weak answer.

"Sadie Rose," she said, "It's me, Lucy. And Ben's with me."

The weak voice sounded a bit stronger. "Oh Lucy, Ben. Please come in."

Lucy opened the door and saw a small chamber that was mostly taken up with a wide chifforobe stuffed full of Sadie's fancy gowns. Lying in the bed with her undone hair flayed across the pillow, Sadie Rose looked small, weak, and vulnerable. There was no paint now, and her cheeks were nearly as pale as the white sheets.

"Lucy," she said, "how I was hoping you'd come. How did you learn I was ill?"

Lucy rushed to her friend's bedside and knelt down to take her hand. "I just now learned. I hadn't seen you and became alarmed, so Ben and I stopped to see. I'm so glad we did."

"Young Ben," Sadie Rose said softly, looking up at him. "So faithful to your cousin." To Lucy, she said, "I know you're not supposed to be here."

Lucy ignored the remark. "Sadie Rose, I heard Mrs. Menessier say something about the rent."

"I wish you hadn't heard." Tears clouded Sadie Rose's eyes. "Perhaps I chose the wrong time to come to Cincinnati. I didn't know times were as hard as they were." She took a deep breath and coughed. Lucy handed her a handkerchief from the nearby table.

"Do you not have enough money for the rent?" Lucy asked.

"I kept up, but just barely, until I fell sick. But now I can't work, and I've fallen behind. Mrs. Menessier tells me she's not running a charity house or a hospital."

"We can bring food," Ben said.

Lucy looked up at Ben and felt like hugging him.

"Of course we can bring food," Lucy agreed. "And we will." She patted Sadie Rose's fever-hot hand. "You rest now and don't worry about a thing. We'll be back!"

When they came back down the stairs, Mrs. Menessier was there to meet them. "If her rent's not paid soon," she said, "I'm notifying the officials at the poorhouse."

Lucy's hand flew to her mouth to stifle the gasp. Sadie Rose taken to the poorhouse! She felt weak in the knees.

But to her surprise, Ben stepped forward. "No need for that just yet," he said, his voice steady. "Give us a couple days to see what can be done on Miss Sadie Rose's behalf."

The hefty lady hesitated. "It's not like I want to be cruel," she said. "But I have to eat, too. And I can't afford to keep a room occupied with someone who cannot pay rent."

"Of course," Ben said. "We understand." He guided Lucy toward the door. "We'll be back shortly."

"What're we going to do, Ben? Do you have a plan?"

"Part of a plan," he said. "Remember the coins Sadie Rose

paid us for carrying her bags the day we met her?"

"Of course," Lucy said. "Are you going to pay her rent with her own coins?"

Ben nodded. "It's probably not enough, but it may suffice to calm Mrs. Menessier and show her we're serious about helping."

"What a wonderful idea."

"You go on home now, Lucy. I'll go back to the boarding house as soon as I get the food and money. I can take a jar of goat's milk and maybe some cornbread."

"But Ben, I want to go with you. I want to help Sadie Rose." They'd arrived at Lucy's front gate, and she was chilled to the bone. Still, she wanted to go back with Ben to the boarding house.

"You can be more help by not worrying your mama." Ben opened the gate. "I promise I'll stop by on my way home and let you know what happened."

There was nothing else she could do, and Lucy knew it. If Mama found out, then Lucy might spoil her chances of doing anything for Sadie Rose.

Later that evening, Ben stopped by the house under the pretense of delivering a cleaned rabbit for Lucy's mama. Before leaving, he slipped Lucy a note. When Lucy went to her room after evening prayers, she drew out the note. Ben had written these words: "Sadie Rose thankful for food. The few coins paid a fraction of the rent due. Mrs. M. may take milk for partial trade. We'll talk tomorrow of further plans."

Lucy sank down on her bed in discouragement. There had to be a way to help. This was a desperate situation. And desperate situations called for desperate measures!

CHAPTER 17
Lucy Takes Action

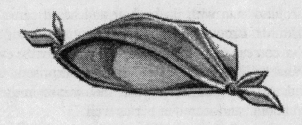

Lucy never undressed for bed that night. She crawled beneath the covers with all her clothes on, waiting for the house to grow quiet. She was determined not to fall asleep.

When all was quiet, she got up and pulled on her heavy woolen cloak, first tying her muffler around her neck. Never before had she disobeyed her parents so blatantly. But she simply had to save Sadie Rose from going to the poorhouse.

With barely a sound, she made her way down the stairs and out the back door into the dark, cold night. Gas lamps were lit at every seventh house, and she found herself scurrying from lamp to lamp. It took all her courage to turn down Front Street. While she'd never been frightened to be there in the daylight, darkness was much different.

Ahead of her loomed the glowing windows of Brooks Tavern. Pulling the cloak more tightly about her, Lucy hurried to the door, where she could hear the shouts and laughter coming from inside. Just as she reached out to open the door, it flew open, and a weaving, staggering man pushed past her, nearly knocking her off her feet.

Taking a breath to muster more courage, she boldly stepped inside the door. Suddenly, the noise subsided and all eyes were on Lucy. Remembering Sadie's dilemma, she flung off her hood and stood as tall as she could. "Mr. Brooks?" she said.

A rotund man with bushy hair and beard came toward her. "I'm Mr. Brooks. What're you doing here, little girl?"

"I've come to take the place of Sadie Rose for the evening."

"What?" Mr. Brooks was at first surprised, then he laughed. All around him the other men joined in the laughter and hooted and jeered at her as well.

"I can play," she said, lifting her voice over the noise. "And I can sing. If you give me a chance, we can all help Sadie Rose." She looked around at the men. "You'd like that, wouldn't you? To help Sadie Rose?"

"Sadie's had a real spell of it. I suppose she does need help." The proprietor of the tavern clawed at his chin whiskers. "Well, I guess it can't hurt." He waved to the piano. "Have a go of it, little girl. Let's see what your voice sounds like."

Lucy removed her cloak and folded it beneath her on the piano stool. It had been several months since she had learned the hymn. Would she remember?

She placed her hands on the keys and began the first few bars of "A Mighty Fortress Is Our God." When the men heard it, one called out, "Say there, this ain't church. Play

132

one of Sadie's songs." But another said, "Shush your mouth. I wanna hear the hymn."

Lucy ignored them all. Once she knew she had the playing down pat, she let loose in her strong clear voice to sing every word. When she finished the last verse, there were hoots and hollers, but now they were in appreciation. "More," they said clapping. "Sing it again."

Lucy reached inside her sleeve for her handkerchief. Tying the corners to make a little pouch, she held it up. "Here's where you put the money for Sadie Rose." As the little hanky-pouch was being passed around the room, she sang the hymn again. This time she was surprised to see several of the men weeping. Maybe she was helping more than Sadie Rose by her singing.

The next day when she told Ben what she'd done, he was shocked. "Lucy, I sometimes think you can never surprise me with your actions, but I'm always wrong. Don't you know you could have been killed down there?"

"I just remembered what Sadie Rose said about the boatmen. If you try to understand people and not act snooty, they respect you." She felt the heavy bag bumping against her leg, where she'd fastened it securely beneath her skirts. "In fact, one of the men walked me to Second Street to make sure I was safe."

Ben just shook his head.

That day after school, they went to the boarding house to pay the money to Mrs. Menessier.

She cast a wary look in their direction when she saw the coins. Although the older woman asked nothing, Lucy was sure she was wondering where two children had come up with that much money. With that payment, Sadie Rose's rent was almost current. They hurried up to her room to tell her.

When Sadie Rose heard of Lucy's escapade, she laughed right out loud. "Lucy Lankford, you are quite a girl." Over and over she thanked them for helping. Propped up against several pillows, Sadie Rose had a little more pink in her cheeks. "I know I'll be better now. In fact, after drinking the tasty goat's milk, my insides are settling down for the first time in days."

Lucy pulled a chair close to the bed. As she did, something fell to the floor. It was a length of blue flowered cloth. Picking it up, Lucy felt her breath catch. "Sadie Rose, what's this piece of cloth?"

Sadie Rose reached out to take the cloth from Lucy. "That," she said, "is a shawl. Or rather, part of a shawl."

"Part?" Lucy scooted her chair closer.

Sadie Rose stroked the cloth tenderly. "It belonged to my ma. I cut it in half when my little brother was taken from me. I kept one half and gave him the other half. Although he was only three, I put it in his tiny fist and said, 'Thomas, don't ever forget me. I'll see you again one day.' "

Lucy suddenly pushed the chair back and stood to her feet. "Well now, we'd really better be going. Mama's expecting me."

"Of course," Sadie Rose replied, "and I'm rather tired from all this excitement." Again she gave her thanks as they left.

"Benjamin Allerton," Lucy said once they were out of the house. "Are you thinking what I'm thinking?"

Ben shook his head. "It can't be."

"But we know that Raggy was an orphan and that his adoptive parents died."

"That's true, but Raggy's name is Russell, not Thomas."

"Maybe the people who adopted him changed his name."

Ben thought about that. "Possibly. But what can we. . .?"

"Don't worry. I have a plan."

Ben laughed. "I'm sure you do, Lucy. I'm sure you do."

But when Lucy arrived home, any plan she'd had was quickly squelched. Once again, she was greeted by a very upset and very disappointed mama. Papa was by her side, and Lucy could tell from their expressions that it was not good.

Papa asked her to come into the parlor, where they could talk.

"Lucy Lankford," Mama began, "I truly thought I'd heard everything. Now I've learned you slipped out of this house in the dead of night and went down to Front Street to a tavern. One of the most dangerous places in all the city. Lucy, how could you disgrace us this way?"

Papa's face mirrored Mama's disappointment. It was enough to break Lucy's heart.

"Mama, Papa, I never wanted to disobey you, but I had to go to the tavern. I had to save Sadie Rose's life. They were threatening to take her to the poorhouse."

"Poorhouse? What are you talking about?" Papa said. "You were told not to see this woman named Sadie Rose."

"I wouldn't have gone to talk to her, but I hadn't seen her in town for two weeks. When we checked on her, we found she was ill with chills and fever." Lucy was wringing her hands and trying not to cry. "Don't you see. I'm only doing what you've always taught me, and that's to reach out and help others. Sadie Rose had no one else. The rent was past due. She even said she was hoping I'd come."

"Whoa," Papa said. "I think it's time to hear this story from beginning to end."

Lucy sat down by the roaring fire and started at the

beginning. She told how Sadie Rose played and sang in taverns so she could earn money to keep searching for her brother. Lucy even had to tell how she went to the tavern to learn how to play the piano, which made Mama wince.

When Lucy finished her story, Papa looked at Mama. "If the church were more generous with their own piano, this might never have happened."

"Paul," Mama said evenly, "we can't blame others for our daughter's disobedience."

"I know I shouldn't have gone," Lucy said. "I was trying to let patience have a perfect work. But I wanted so just to learn a song. And now I can play a hymn all the way through. When I played the hymn for the men at the tavern. . ."

"You played a hymn at the tavern?" Papa interrupted.

Lucy nodded, and she saw Papa smile.

"When I played the hymn," she continued, "the men were crying. I think men in a tavern need a hymn, don't you, Papa?"

"They surely do," he agreed.

"Paul," Mama said in a warning tone.

"And Sadie Rose needs hymns, too," Lucy said, talking faster. "I believe if some of our church ladies would visit her rather than talking about her all the time, she might just come to church." Lucy remembered how pleased Sadie Rose had been when Lucy had prayed for her. "I think she truly wants to have God's forgiveness."

"Well," Mama said slowly, as though she were thinking it through. "I suppose I could take a couple ladies with me from the church and call on Miss Sadie Rose tomorrow."

Lucy jumped up from her chair. "Oh, would you, Mama? Would you go there after school so I can meet you there? Then I could introduce you to Sadie Rose."

"I'll see if I can arrange that."

"But you, young lady, will still be punished for your disobedience," Papa reminded her. "Not only did you disobey our direct instructions, but I'm also disappointed that you didn't feel you could trust us enough to tell us about the situation and work with us to solve Sadie Rose's problems. You could have been very badly hurt last night. First Street is not a safe place for a woman, much less a young girl."

"I'm sorry," Lucy said. "I should have told you everything from the beginning."

In the end, Mama and Papa set up a list of jobs for Lucy to do every evening after school for a week.

The next day, Lucy could barely sit still in the classroom. The large clock mounted in front of the room moved at a snail's pace. At recess she was distracted and barely listened to a word Charlotte was saying, even though Charlotte was reporting good news about her father. She said her father had been able to secure a loan from another city and was making plans to start a new business. In spite of the encouraging news, Lucy could think only about Sadie and Raggy. Could Raggy actually be Sadie's long-lost brother?

As soon as school let out, Lucy hurried outside to meet up with Ben.

"We'll head down to Sausage Row first," Lucy said.

"I hope you're right about this, Lucy. How'll we find Mabel Peattie's place?"

"Easy. We just ask. In Sausage Row, everybody knows everybody."

"But what if Raggy won't listen to us?"

"I don't expect him to."

"You're not making any sense."

"Just follow me and do what I say."

Winter had been especially cruel to the poverty-stricken areas around the landing. The shacks seemed more dilapidated than ever. As Lucy had thought, it was easy to find where the washerwoman lived. But would Raggy be there?

As they approached the small house with its little lean-to in the back, Lucy saw Raggy. He was taller and more wiry-looking than ever. She'd almost forgotten how long it had been since she'd seen him. Suddenly, she wondered if her plan would work. But it was too late to back out.

"When he comes after us," she whispered to Ben, "you go one way and I'll go the other. Lead him to the boarding house."

"What a crazy plan," Ben said, grinning at her.

"Hey, Raggy!" she called out. "Still carry your rag with you wherever you go?"

Raggy looked around to see where the voice came from. When he spied them, he spouted, "Why you. . ."

Ben shouted out, "Rag-gee, Rag-gee. Carries his rags with him wherever he goes."

The plan worked like a charm. Raggy was on their heels like a pup after a rabbit. Lucy ran straight up Broadway, while Ben ducked down a side street. As Lucy had expected, Raggy went after Ben.

When she hit the front door of the boarding house, Lucy didn't stop to knock. There in the front parlor sat Mama and Widow Tuthill and two other ladies.

"Come on," she called out, panting and puffing. "Let's go meet Sadie Rose."

"Lucy. . ." Mama started.

"Your daughter is a little ruffian," Widow Tuthill interrupted haughtily.

From behind her, Lucy heard Mama say, "She's just a little more energetic than most girls."

When Sadie Rose answered her knock, Lucy was pleased to see her up and dressed and sitting by the fire in her Boston rocker.

"Sadie, I've brought company," Lucy said, waving the ladies in and then running to the window to see if Ben had arrived.

"Lucy," Mama said, "what are you doing?"

"Mama, I'd like you to meet Sadie Rose." Lucy motioned toward her mama, but kept looking out the window. Just as she'd introduced all the ladies, Ben came speeding into the alleyway behind the boarding house.

"Sadie Rose, quick. Where's the shawl?"

"The what?"

"The shawl. The shawl your ma left to you. Hurry." Lucy had no way of knowing how closely Raggy was following Ben.

Sadie stood and walked across the room to her bed. From beneath the pillow she pulled out the cloth. "It's here."

Lucy took it from her hand and flung open the window. Raggy had arrived and was squaring off with Ben, his fists upraised.

"Raggy Wallace," she called out. Raggy looked up at her.

"Wallace?" Sadie said. She moved to the window beside Lucy. "That's my name. Wallace."

"Russell Wallace," Lucy said this time, using his real name and waving the piece of shawl. "Does this look familiar?"

Raggy stared, unable to move.

Ben, who'd had his fists in the air, backed away, looking more than a little relieved.

Slowly, Raggy reached inside his threadbare shirt, drew

out the piece of faded cloth, and held it forth like a flag of surrender.

"Thomas?" Sadie Rose asked softly. "Russell Thomas Wallace?"

"Sadie Rose?" came Raggy's small voice. "Is that really you?"

Sadie Rose turned to look at Lucy. "Oh, Lucy! You were right! We prayed and God heard. He truly heard." With that she flew out the door and down the stairs into the snow, not bothering to grab a cloak.

Within moments, the ladies from church witnessed the tearful reunion of the long-separated brother and sister. And there wasn't a dry eye or hankie among them.

CHAPTER 18

Steamboat's Coming!

In spite of her very grown-up-looking new dress and matching bonnet, Lucy could hardly contain her excitement as she stood on the landing waiting for the *Velocipede* to come into view. The winter snows had melted, the spring rains had fallen, and the majestic Ohio flowed full and wide once again.

Lucy looked over at Sadie Rose, and they exchanged smiles. The arrival of the new piano meant that Sadie Rose would begin giving piano lessons in the front parlor of the Lankford home. That had been Lucy's idea. But Mama had had the wonderful idea to hire Mabel Peattie as their servant.

Papa and George had completed one of their steamboats and the buyer was able to make a partial payment. Papa said that was agreeable because as soon as the boat was launched and in business, the owner would be able to pay the balance. Now the second boat was nearing completion.

Ben and Thomas stood off to the side, talking about steamboats. It had been hard to stop saying Raggy and to remember to say Tom or Thomas. But Lucy didn't mind taking the extra effort to learn. Now that Tom was clean, wore nice clothes, and had enough to eat, he didn't look like the same boy. Since Ben understood about being an orphan, he and Thomas had become fast friends.

Lucy and Ben had learned that Tom was fascinated with Milliken and wanted more than anything to learn to milk the goat. Lucy marveled as she thought about it. That day at the church when he'd tried to take Milliken, he'd only wanted to pet her.

Lucy realized she'd been as wrong about Raggy as her mama had been about Sadie Rose. They'd all learned a lesson in love.

Suddenly, someone far up the landing shouted, "Steamboat's a-comin'!" The call echoed up and down the public landing and Lucy started jumping up and down in spite of herself.

Papa had rented a sturdy wagon, and it was sitting nearby. At last the proud white boat came into view with its twin black smokestacks pointing skyward.

Presently, the boat was docked and Captain Saffins strode down the gangplank to greet them. "It's been a long time," he said, laughing and shaking Papa's hand.

"Yes, Captain. A long time," Papa answered. "We've all learned how to be patient." He glanced at Lucy and winked.

Then Lucy watched as the stevedores guided the crane that lifted the crate containing her piano. Slowly, slowly, it came over to where Papa lined up the wagon. Slowly, slowly, it was let down into the back of the wagon. Lucy didn't breathe until it was safely settled. Ben and Thomas climbed into the wagon to hold the crate steady. They seemed almost as excited about the arrival as Lucy.

"May I ride home in the wagon with you, Papa?" Lucy asked.

"Why, of course, Little Lucy. Excuse me. I mean, why of course, Miss Lucy. May I give you a hand up?" Papa bowed and offered his hand.

As the others boarded the waiting carriage, Lucy allowed Papa to assist her into the wagon seat. Papa climbed up beside her, shook the reins, and told the team to "Giddap." Lucy straightened her full skirts, adjusted her bonnet, and opened her ruffled parasol to protect her face from the bright spring sunshine.

The wagon clattered over the cobblestones of the landing, taking the new piano home.

Good News for Readers

There's more! The American Adventure continues with *Escape from Slavery*. Tim Allerton is angry. At school, Hollis Bodley is trying to outdo Tim in everything and openly makes fun of Tim's antislavery views. At home Tim's father is constantly reminding him to keep his opinions to himself because their family business is dependent on customers from the South. Pam, Tim's younger sister, doesn't understand why he has a problem with slavery in the first place. "Slaves are treated just like family," she says.

Then Tim and Pam are put in a situation where they can save the life of an escaped slave baby whose mother has just been killed. Will Pam change her views on slavery. . . or will she continue to ignore the problem? And when a move to drive black people out of the section of the city called "Little Africa" puts the life of Tim's good friend Ward Baker in danger, how will he be able to help?